D0375856

Other novels by Curt Leviant

The Yemenite Girl
Passion in the Desert
The Man Who Thought He Was Messiah

PARTITA
IN
VENICE

PARTITA

in

Venice

a novel by

CURT LEVIANT

Livingston Press
at
The University of West Alabama

ISBN 0-942979-64-8, cloth
ISBN 0-942979-63-X, paper

Library of Congress Catalog Number: 99-64440

*This is a work of imagination, and so the characters and events in the book are
fictitious. Any resemblance to people living, in a state of limbo, or in the con-
tinuum in between that most folk find themselves in, is plain happenstance or
downright (since you're expecting the word) coincidence.*

Manufactured in the United States of America.

Printed by Patterson Printing
Hardcover binding by Heckman Bindery
Typesetting and layout by Joe Taylor
Cover Design by Curt Leviant and Joe Taylor
Cover: detail of Antonio Canaletto's "Venice, Palazzo Ducale, "
        used with permission of Corel Professional Photos, 3 Rivers
Proofreading: Tina N. Jones, Curt Leviant, Stephanie Parnell, Joe Taylor, and Jill
        Wallace

"Specializing in offbeat & Southern literature"
Livingston Press
Station 22
The University of West Alabama
Livingston, AL 35470

Beginning

1. Zoe...5
2. How Much He Loved Venice...................................8
3. First Love...11
4. Double Disappearance..15
5. Hero Meets Heroine...20
6. How Long Is a Long Wait?..................................26
7. The Meaning of Dreams......................................29
8. What He Does, What She Does, What They Did..........33
9. Happy's Will Power..................................38
10. The Fickle Color of Her Hair...............................42
11. Who Fills His Days, Who Fills His Thoughts..............45

Middle

1. Tasting Life More Than Once.................................55
2. The Atom That Defied Newton..........................57
3. Any Secrets?....................64
4. On Becoming Invisible...68
5. The Mirror...77
6. Happy Flirtatious, Happy on Fire............................79
7. How Sweet the Feeling When the Fight Is Forgotten..........83
8. Face to Face with the Secret................................89
9. When the Phone Rings Tranquility Is Broken...................90
10. Why Tommy Was in Venice.........................97
11. The Yellow Umbrellas in the Rockefeller Center Rink..........101
12. Perpetuo Mobile of Memories..........................105
13. The Eternal Question......................................108
14. Up in the Bell Tower......................................112
15. When You Take A Girl to a Luxury Hotel Is That a Sign of Love?.116
16. Meet You by the Fountain, Third Sunday in July.........120
17. I'd Love To See a Picture!................................123

End

1. Who Is More Sarcastic?..................127
2. Tall Aunt Maria and the Amazing St. Bernard...............133
3. Guess Who's the Gondolier?..............141
4. The Pigeon as Messenger......146
5. Partita and Its Baker's Dozen Definitions............157
6. Up in the Bell Tower, Again.....................168
7. Running Until He Bumps Into Di Rossi............171
8. Where'd You Disappear To?.................182
9. About Face.....................................188
10. What the Pocketbook Had To Say.................194
11. Sunrise.................................199

For Erika
lovelier than Venice

BEGINNING

1. *Zoe*

"Zoe."

That's what she said when he asked her name, saying it with a shy downward glance, as if she couldn't bear looking into his eyes for too long. But he looked at her. Even though she was on her haunches, gathering—with his help—the items that had fallen out of her knapsack, he sculpted her with his glance. He looked at her wavy brown hair, curved his gaze around her butt, zigzagged up to her bare thighs and knees, then coasted down her legs to her sneakers.

She seemed pleased that the room was noisy again; the silence she had created a few minutes earlier, broken. No longer was she the center of attention. The crowd in the American Express office had other things to do. Like watch the gondolas or hang out in Piazza San Marco.

"I always wondered what's in a girl's pocketbook," he said, picking up her fallen drugstore. "Now I know what's in her knapsack . . . ten pocketbooks!"

Zoe, she said.

Zoe, he thought as he scanned her again like lines on a page, reading her from left to right, enjoying the paragraphs of her body.

But the name was rather odd. Zoe. Heavy in its gravity, that bottom-of-ladder Z; downended like the low part of a see-saw. Who nowadays had names that began with Z? Girls were called Ann and Brenda, Cheryl and Debbie. Loads and loads of Debbies. If you forgot a salesgirl's name, odds were if you said, Debbie, you got your girl. Ginny too. Most names floated to the upper ranges of the alphabet. You rarely ran across an Ursula or Veronica. Maybe a Wendy or two. But at the bottom of the finite scale of letters, beyond which there were none?Names with Z? Never. Zelda had gone out with the Fitzgeralds.

Zoe.

He liked the surprise of the name. Even more, the music of the name.

Zoe.

To counterbalance the gravity of the alphabetical location— he tilted the see-saw up, way up—was its light vibrato, its airiness, soft and smooth as down.

Zoe.

No heavy consonants. One musical initial sound and two vowels, like notes in a song. The Z, he remembered reading, was the least used letter in the alphabet, E the most, O a close second. Her name, then, contained polar ends, inverting into itself, like a bent mirror. He didn't share with her his analysis but did admit he liked the name. On second thought, maybe he *did* tell her once about the letters of her name. Then again, perhaps all this rumination did not come until much later.

Long ago that was. But memories, like old love, neither age nor fade away. A plow may rust, went the Vermont farmers' saying his father loved to repeat, but never old friendship. And now he was in Venice again for the Festa del Redentore, just two weeks away. What did he do to pass the time? Early morning breakfast, a walk in the calles, delighting in the sound of footfalls echoing in the tight alleys, cappuccino on the Piazza. Sometimes, to be ornery, a full cup of tea, staring at the meniscus until he saw Zoe in it and then sipped it away. Reading the *International Herald Tribune* and *Il Veneziano*. Making faces at himself in the mirror. Maybe lunch or just gelato, then two excursions, one by land, one by water. Dinner at a small trattoria and a concert at night, usually Vivaldi, Venice's own son, at one of the churches or Scuole. Gliding like a gondola through the hours, sweeping the days away with his oars. Waiting for the Festa, that glorious third Sunday in July when all Venice was ablaze at night with lights so bright that night was lighter than day; when gondolas formed a mile-long chain, a bridge across the Giudecca Canal to the Redentore Church, and each gondola was lit by colored lights; when song and music drifted from every window, and drink and dance were everywhere, and Venetians at the end of the night went to the Lido to watch the sunrise to mark the end of the Festa celebration. And within him too light would sing and end with fireworks that would reflect the sunburst within him when he and Zoe were together those beautiful days, years and years ago. The Festa that would soon be here again, like phases of the moon, like Mercury around the sun, each at its own pace, in its own time.

He wanted to write down his feelings at being back in Venice and what he hoped to do here but could not because the city's sights seduced him, those twice-a-day excursions, and he kept putting it off. He felt this tension flowing through his veins, a restrained kinetic buzz, untranslatable to any known set of words or metaphors. Was it a spiritual hunger waiting for the daily feeding? Anticipation? A pot of gold at rainbow's end? Another Zoe perhaps? It was just a matter of time, he promised himself, and he would sit down to the enjoyable task of shaping his ideas.

2. How Much He Loved Venice

He loved walking in the city. No matter how long a walk was in Venice, all of which could be traversed by foot, it was always shorter the second time. In fact, the more one walked a certain route, the shorter it became. But after three days he found himself floating. For him, being in Venice was like entering a photograph, exploring behind the image, and finding a magic portal to where no one had ever set foot before.

One of the first things he would do on his annual pilgrimages to Venice was to walk—he could have done it blindfolded—to the American Express. The office had hardly changed. Maybe a few computer screens added. But the space was still the same. He stayed to look at the mostly young people coming and going. What did he expect to find, a young girl entering and while unslinging her dark green knapsack, it drops to the floor and the flaps, thought to be secure, betrayed their owner's intent and, true to their name, flapped open and out came the sack's socks and salves, and dots and specks of tiny sundries? Did he really expect a scenario like that again? No. There was only one Zoe in this world and what happened once could never happen again.

His father, quoting a writer he had once read—he could not recall precisely who—had called Venice "unique and fabulously different." But that was obvious. You didn't have to be a writer to come to that conclusion.

He arrived by boat, per his father's suggestion, to get the full panoply of Venice pulled toward him by an invisible tow. For a first seeing it was imperative to view the city properly. A second time you could come from anywhere; it didn't matter. But a first visit was special. Of course, entering Piazza San Marco from a narrow lane and seeing the great square opening up like a magical sunrise wasn't bad either. The designers of the city had purposely made the access lanes narrow so that a walker would emerge into the light of the Piazza and take in, like an insuck of breath, its vast open space and its gem and lace diversity.

But from the sea, from the sea you saw it as Canaletto and other artists had painted it, as sailors and conquerors saw it, as merchants and travelers through the ages beheld it, coming into view like drapes slowly being opened. Approach by sea the city built on water and be in harmony with its ancient spirit.

But he had no illusions about the city. For all its beauty, it had its dross. The gondolas, the palazzos, San Marco were pearls on the crown; but the weather, the winds, the smells from the canals, the detritus on the Piazza, all were antipodes to the beauty, omitted from the picture postcards and the works of art.

It was the silence of Venice that he loved the most, the strange silence of a gondola in the water, the heart of silence of a calle at night. He wished he could find more words for "quiet." When asked why he liked Venice, he said: "I'm a country boy from Vermont and I love quiet. I like Venice because it doesn't have cars." The joke had a kernel of truth, however, for when he visited Florence, where traffic, especially motorcycle and scooter noise, wound an unending ribbon of roars around the city, he appreciated Venice all the more and couldn't wait to get back. But in Venice even sounds were soothing. Heels clacking on the cobblestones at dawn; at vespers, the churchbells. The hum of people strolling on the Lista de Spagna till all hours of the night.

The absence of car noise, he discovered, enhances all other sounds. In Venice, conversation seemed clearer without the swoosh and hum of traffic. One heard the water lapping the edges of the shore, the oars of the gondola cutting the water. Venice sunshine is unfiltered; silence makes it brighter. The people were different too; more relaxed than in Rome. And stronger. Miles and miles of walking and lugging toughen leg and arm muscles; that's why women push baby carriages up and down, thump-a-thump, the steps of the bridges with ease and grace.

And so, his first three days in Venice—if constant exposure to beauty may be so termed—were uneventful.

Until one day, wham, it hit him unexpectedly, like it had years ago here. As he stood by the quay on the Riva degli Schiavone, around the corner from the Doge's Palace, his back to the Danieli Hotel, he saw her sailing away on a vaporetto, on Line 52.

He had just missed the boat, which read as a pun if you wish. She stood on the deck next to the conductor. Like in a book, like in the movies, the sun shone through her blonde hair. Or maybe it was a spotlight. He didn't know a lot of things, but what he did know was that the vaporetto was pulling away. Goodbye, Blondie, forever. Again the subway syndrome. A girl stands on a platform. The train pulls in. He watches her enter. He sees the doors close. She turns around. The train starts to move. He looks at her; she at him. Their eyes do not waver. Love at first sight. Wait, he shouts to himself. That's my destined bride. Until the train vanishes into the tunnel forever. Ditto, here. Except that in Venice it's the vaporetto syndrome. Like vapor, gone. Another true love lost. Vanishing in the waves.

3. First Love

This was not his first love in Venice. There was another, we know by now. Exactly twenty-five years ago. Just before the Festa del Redentore. He knew the date precisely. How could he forget?

It happened the first time he came to Venice, July of 1967, when he had just turned twenty-two. In June, like many of his friends who had graduated from Dartmouth, he took the summer off to travel around Europe. Venice was damp and chill the mid-July day he arrived, and in the crowded Piazza he tried to imagine what it was like in spring when it was quiet, devoid of tourists. For two long days he was alone, as lonely as a scarecrow in a sorghum field. He had no interest in striking up friendship, avoided the popular sport of café pickups more out of shyness than disdain, although he persuaded himself it was a romantic aloofness that kept him keeping his own company.

But all that changed on his third day in Venice. It happened in the American Express office as it might have happened in the movies. And like in the films, a stance, a habit, a way of life suddenly alters direction when a woman enters the scene. He was on line waiting to change some travelers checks. The door slammed, loudly —or perhaps it was loud only now in his memory. He turned, just in time to see a girl coming in with a scruffy old green knapsack on her back, looking as confused as a newcomer at a party where everyone is socializing and seems to know everyone else, where everyone is apparently paired off except the dithered gal in the doorway.

Her attire, her accouterments, declared she was well off. Only the rich would slum it like her, he thought, with that green canvas knapsack like a soldier from World War Two. As she eased the old khaki bag from her shoulder, it seemed to lurch forward of its own accord. Down to the floor it fell, spilling its contents. Out flew a dozen or two vials and notions, phials and lotions, brushes and potions. Soaps and suntan creams, pills to sweeten dreams, jimble-jambled over small plastic bottles of shampoo squirreled away from hotels that pretended to elegance, none of which could possibly have helped make her any prettier.

For she was plain of face was Zoe, no denying that. She herself

realized it, for once, later, when she noted how long it took someone to react to her knapsack spill, she said, If I were gorgeous,
everyone would have rushed to help me. But they see a fair-to-
middlin girl, so why bother? Nonsense, he protested, I ran over to
you, pretty as a picture. Neither photos nor nostalgia could alter
her plain Jane face—but her body had it over her face five to one.
Slim, well-tapered legs—she wore khaki shorts—a thin waist and
superb breasts. When she moved, her upper torso moved on its
own. There was subtle independence to this movement, a harmony that attracted eye, not ear. Nevertheless, he had to admit
that he heard a sensual ringing in his ears when he looked at her,
the whole of her, not just her face, because she was even more than
the sum of her parts.

At first he saw that the people who looked at her were embarrassed at her distress. They were annoyed at her breaking the code
of invincibility of youth and its utter sophistication, confidence,
élan. He joined the crowd in snubbing her lack of social grace, her
clumsiness. The nerve of her drawing attention to herself away
from what everyone was doing— chatting, cashing checks, laughing, reading mail. The crowd staring at her seemed to send the
message: serves you right for breaking the spell. At first he was
with them on the other side of the line, but then a pang of sorrow
flowed through him—he saw her distress, her embarrassment—
and he switched sides. He took one look at this innocent-faced girl
bending down to retrieve soap, little boxes of eye care, packets of
film, and at once walked over to her, bent down opposite her, and
helped her scoop up her stuff.

And while both were on their haunches, his face close to hers,
he asked her, "What's your name?"

She said, "Zoe. And yours?"

"Tommy. Thomas Manning."

"That was very sweet of you to come and help me," she said
later over a cappuccino, the first she'd ever drunk. "Everyone else
was just staring. God, I felt so awful, so clumsy."

"So alone."

"Yes. How did you know?"

"I can put myself into other people's sneakers. It's like magic."

"It certainly is. It's very rare. And I admire you for it . . . God,
I felt so humiliated. As if I was onstage and tripped and everyone's

eyes were on me."

"People *were* staring."

"I would almost say that some of them were glad something like that happened. It gave them something to gloat about, don't you think?"

"There's a term, in German of course, for that feeling of joy at someone else's distress, but I forget it now."

"Me, if I see that happening to someone I do everything I can, and quickly too, to help him."

"Me too," he said.

"And you did. Thanks."

He took her hand and pressed it, as if to say: I'm glad I did; I did it for you; and other things that only fingers can express and mouths haven't yet learned to articulate.

"I feel sorry for people," he told her, wondering if his words didn't ring hollow or pretentious. "That's the way I am. I suffer the woes of mankind. Every plane crash, untimely death, even obituaries of strangers affect me. I sigh. Commiserate. Utter a few heartfelt tsk-tsks." Then he shifted timbre, expression, saying it lightly, in an almost ironical tone so as not to sound insufferable. "But I realize it's a sham. It doesn't affect me at all." He looked at Zoe to see the effect his words were having. "It's just a knee-jerk reaction. How do I know? you ask, even though you don't ask but I can see the question mark leaping like a beam of light from your eyes. For you're surprised, absolutely astonished, at the turn of my remarks. How do I know it doesn't affect me? Because when I get a tiny paper cut on my finger that takes days to heal and sends out a minuscule ray of pain, it bothers me more than all the plane tragedies and war victim photos and world calamities I read about in papers or see on tv."

She accepted this—even his change of stance—without a word. Only later did she say, "I thought about what you said and I feel you're being hard on yourself. I can't imagine you insensitive. The way you came to help me shows me what you're really like."

"Like as if I was quoting myself out of context," he said, knowing he was sounding absurd.

"Maybe. Something like that. So don't feel bad. It's human nature."

"I don't feel bad at all," he said. "So why make me feel guilty?"

Zoe was silent for a moment, surprised at the rough edge of his remark.

"On the contrary," she said softly. "I'm not trying to make you feel guilty. I'm trying to console you, convince you that you shouldn't feel guilty. I'm trying to make you feel good. So why turn the tables on me?"

"*Schadenfreude*," he said.

"What?"

"That's the German word for delight at someone else's sorrow. Schaden, by the way, was Freud's original first name; then he changed it to Sigmund."

When years later he repeated his paper-cut speech (after all, how many ideas are there in a man's skull that don't get recycled a number of times?) to another girl, she said:

"Then you're not as sweet as you make yourself to be."

"I said what I said," was his assertive response, "hiding nothing, making myself out to be neither this nor that. Only human."

The girl had no retort. But he mouthed for her a response that she might have made had she the tongue for it. "Being human is miracle enough."

4. Double Disappearance

Including everything in Venice, all of which is *miracoloso*, the existence of the city and what happens in it. And since miracles, as Emerson said, are daily events, he was only mildly surprised, but of course exceedingly delighted—although ecstatic might be a better word—to see the vaporetto Blondie sitting at the nearly empty Florian's café early the next morning, as if waiting for him. Destiny's daughter.

First she disappeared and now—there she was de-evanesced at an adjoining table. Apparently, she hadn't ordered yet. There was nothing before her except a small black tray. Twice a waiter approached and she said something softly in English—perhaps that she was expecting someone—and away he went. She kept looking at her watch and shaking her head, as if silently berating the guy, it had to be a guy, he thought, although it could have been a girlfriend; he would have preferred the latter, but his heart told him that with her looks and shape it had to be the former, who kept her waiting. Or was all this a show and she's waiting to be picked up? He kept looking at her until she finally turned his way. She was young, probably a college kid on summer vacation, twenty or twenty-one, with pink jutting lips, like models have in lipstick ads, lips slightly parted that beckoned; kiss me, I have kissable lips, so kiss me; lips that even in photographs seem three-dimensional. She gave him a movie smile, not fixing her gaze on his face but moving her head gradually as she smiled, panning off into the San Marco distance, as though her smile, not directed at him, had accidentally grazed his face.

But they did, thought he, exchange glances. How he loved that phrase! To play with its multi-faceted imagicality, its colloquial imagique. He puts his glance on a piece of paper, she puts hers on the small black tray on her table. They both rise, bow in European fashion with head slightly inclined. He presents his glance on the paper to her, she gives him hers on the tray. Glances exchanged. Officially, at the current rate of. If they're too shy, the waiter intermediates, but all glances are final: no returns, no refunds, no credit, no further exchanges.

And while fantasizing this semantic *reductio ad absurdum*, he doesn't notice that the chair at the adjoining table is now empty. Fool, he says to himself, leaping up. He pays the waiter and dashes off in the direction he assumes she has gone. Oh, if only she had lost a handkerchief like women do in operas, or forgotten her purse on the table, perhaps a pen on the chair. But the only thing she left behind was an extra glance she'd forgotten to exchange, impalpable part of her presence that he hoped he could capture, not return. What else had she left on the chair? he thinks as walls and bridges breeze by. An invisible cutout of herself. But it wasn't her presence he was after. It was her. Yes, today she had sat here with that slim waist and well-filled blue tee shirt that highlighted the blue of her eyes. Who knows if there would be a tomorrow? Perhaps she was only on a three-day visit, like most tourists, with no tomorrow. So he plowed on, proud of his decisiveness, running ahead, quicker than the cobblestones rushing the other way, until he caught sight of her twenty feet ahead of him. Now he slowed, followed her discreetly past a quay, in and out of the maze of blind alleys until she stopped at a pensione off a small square. Now his determination wilted. Should he go in? Rooted to the cobblestones by his indecision, he wondered how to pursue further. He sat down at the edge of the fountain. Some people, he knew, are creatures of habit—she was American judging by the few words she had exchanged with the waiter. Perhaps she'd return to the same café.

As he stood she reappeared. She looked at him, passed him, and then—was he distracted by a commotion to his left: two young boys fighting over a bicycle, or a bug in his ear, index finger shaking and scratching there?—then, when he looked again, she was gone. No longer there. Vanished. Disappeared into thin air.

But Zoe, although no longer with him, was always there. No matter how much she wasn't there, she was really there. How come he couldn't erase her from his memory? That scene at Amexco is like a film that can continually be recalled. Her sweet face flustered as she tries to right herself and gather her spilled belongings into that hand-me-down sack. What was it about her that enchanted him, enthralls him still? A sweetness one can't find today. A gentleness he loved; her eagerness to please. Her Mid-West openness, naiveté. She related to everyone, he remembered, with such shyness. Zoe was so small-town timid, timid and pavid, she was even obsequious to waiters and shop personnel. He watched her in restaurants and stores, shy to the point of being apologetic. She let the waiter set the tone; he suggested, offered advice. If something was cold that should have been hot, she wouldn't send it back. "It's okay," she would say. "I don't want to make a fuss." A tepid drink was all right with her too. "Ask him for some ice," he'd tell her. But no. "I don't mind," she'd say. Waiters knew how to palm off yesterday's or the day before that's cakes on her. That little self-effacingness, in exact key signature to the way she'd sidled into Amexco, had electric waves to it. Waiters and shopkeepers, their antennas on high, immediately tuned in.

"You're so shy," he said in a tone of near complaint. "Do you have any other flaws?"

"I'm also absentminded," and gave a self-deprecating laugh.

"Like Einstein?"

"If you say so . . . I forget to eat unless I'm reminded."

"That's exactly what they say about Einstein."

"I can go without eating all day and into the next, unless someone reminds me to eat."

"I'll remind you," he said.

But when she reads, Zoe said, put a bowl of grapes, even two pounds of them, into a bowl before her and, without looking, she could polish off the entire bowl down to the last grape without even noticing.

But after getting to know her, he realized his first judgment of her—that she was well off—was wrong. That beaten-up knapsack wasn't emblematic; it had no subtext. She just couldn't afford anything better. She was only the daughter of a postal clerk, had saved her money dime by dime until, after working a year, she could make her poorman's grand tour. But don't judge a girl by her father. Despite only two years of college, after which she had to go to work, she was well read. She surprised him with her knowledge of *The Aspen Papers* and other books set in Venice. She'd done her homework, that kid.

"And you?" she asked, her eyes wide and bright. "Any flaws?"

He remembered how he loved to watch her when he spoke about himself. Her hand in his, her eyes jumping from his mouth to his eyes.

"None that I can think of. No big city imperfections. I'm just a country boy. I grew up in northern Vermont, which is so rural, so Vermont, we consider the farmers from down in southern Vermont big city fellers. Imagine! I never heard traffic as a kid. Our house was far removed from roads. We saw shooting stars in the summer going in an arc from one end of the sky to the other. When there's no cars you can appreciate the night sky more. And rainbows too, from one pot of gold to the other. You can get up in the morning, see the cows grazing, see the sky forming a complete hemisphere. And not a soul around. You could walk on the paths that led to the tertiary roads that led to the secondary roads and not see a living soul or a car. But Venice is the exact opposite of rural life. Venice is hustle, trade, and transport. It's art, artifice, artificiality. Here everything, except the water, is at a remove from nature. You hardly see a tree, except in the Giardino and a couple of smaller parks. It's art versus nature, the earth versus sea. Maybe it's this tension of opposites that attracts me. Can you see how opposite this city is? I remember sitting at dusk and well into starlight on the portico of our house in Vermont and hearing only the crickets and cicadas late in August, and nothing else. I heard the soft moonbeams landing on our roof with cats' paws. If I made that up, fine. If not, credit good memory."

He stopped, letting the effect sink in.

"I love to hear you talk," Zoe said. "I feel like I'm in the country with you when you talk."

"And in the morning, the crowing of the cock and lowing of the cows. You couldn't find an art gallery or a piano for miles. You'd have to travel hours for a bookshop or a library, I mean a decent one. The smells of the earth and stable clung to me. But my part of the country drives America's food engine. It's amazing that I can blend earth and art. It's because my parents, unlike other farmers, were educated folk. They made a conscious decision after college, to go into organic dairy farming, one of the first in Vermont. But can you see how Venice is created not from nature but totally by man? There's nothing in it except water and even that is controlled by artificial means. When my father would visit, he liked to think that his coming here was a fusion of nature and art. He'd spend three weeks in Europe just before the harvest in June, most of it here. He had a sophisticated taste in architecture, loved Venice, which he considered one of the glories of the civilized world. And he instilled in me, his son, a love of the place long before I first set foot in it. Once here, I felt it was a dream homecoming. I was so sure I had been here before, and indeed, in a way, I had. But, strangely, every time I return, it's as if it's the first time I've been here."

Yes, Venice kept reappearing. But what good was a city without women who made it real? Zoe was gone and that blonde on the vaporetto had disappeared. Again.

Let's see.

5. Hero Meets Heroine

Or did it happen this way?

She sat at one table, he at another, perhaps not at Florian's but a less expensive café. Who's betting that something will click? In Venice the—despite the unseen movie cameras—stage was always the same. It just revolved a bit. Same the Piazza, same the pigeons, tourists too. Canaletto's paintings of Venice could have been today's photos. Nothing was different. Except maybe the coffee was fresher, the waiters too. Would a waiter spill a cup of coffee over her table-cloth, prompting him to rush forward gallantly with a napkin as the movie camera, in a perfectly angled shot, captures both his swift reaction and the spreading brown stain on the white linen? Would she trip over one of those cumbersome wrought iron chairs? Would they bump into each other as both made their way to the arcade, with profuse apologies leading to an exchange of glances which, according to protocol, leads to an exchange of names? (Details, see *supra*). The bad news was that none of the above was happening. The good news was that not only was she alone but between sips of coffee she looked his way only to shift away quickly as if she were scanning the entire scene, not even admitting to herself, much less to him, that he was the object of her gaze. Before assessing what impression his move would make, he got up, pulled out a chair opposite hers, leaned on it, and before she had a chance to turn away, which would have turned him off at once, said quickly:

"Hi, did you ever see a movie where the hero meets the hero-ine because she's just tumbled off her bike on the corner of 14th Street and 2nd Avenue in New York , or slipped on the ice in Rockefeller Center and he helps her up, or she's just parachuted onto the great lawn in Central Park and he helps her fold her yellow chute, or she comes into the American Express here holding her knapsack which falls and all her belongings fall out and no one, not a soul except our hero, budges to help the poor girl scoop up her things and he falls madly in love with her?

And before the surprised girl even had a chance to answer—he noticed she'd brought her cup midway to her mouth and just left it there—he continued:

"But since we're not in New York or Amexco and no one's fallen," except me, thought he, "and I see that you're sitting by yourself and so am I, and we're not strangers, oh no, not by a long shot, for I saw you sailing away on the vaporetto the other day near the Hotel Danieli, you were looking right at me and I was wondering if I'd ever see you again, and you see, so I have, so I have, and now that I have seen you again, maybe it was you at Florian's yesterday who I exchanged glances with and followed through the calles to her pensione and then she disappeared before my eyes like a mirage that fades, and then again, maybe it wasn't you, but today I see that you are the you who was on that vaporetto, no denying that, so now that I've seen you again I was wondering how to begin talking to you so that you shouldn't slip away from me again, not that it's so likely on dry land and café chairs not being gondolas they haven't been known to sail on St. Mark's Square in the entire history of Venice, and so I *am* talking to you, what's your name?" the exact same phrase he used years ago, without the lengthy prolegomenon, when he had met another girl quite by accident in Venice, and he rose, stuck out his hand to shake Blondie's. But when she put out her right hand, he took it with his left hand and held it for a moment. It was an amicable gesture and this too surprised her, he saw.

"Happy," she said and smiled, signaling that what he had done and said was all right with her.

"I'm so glad," he said. "So am I. That's a first for me. Not acquainted with me two minutes and already happy."

"I was Happy before I met you."

"Oh," he said sadly, "and now that you've met me the happiness has disappeared."

"Not at all," and she laughed. "now that I met you I'm still Happy."

"Then that makes me happy too."

"Hardly. But your being whoever you are makes me no less Happy." She paused. "Which happens to be my name... And you?"

"I'm happy too," he said, "but the outside world calls me Tom. Tommy Manning."

"Hi," she said. "Nice to meet you."

"I liked the Shakespearean punning," he said.

For a while there was an awkward silence. Perhaps the Elizabethan reference passed her by. A Venetian silence, where a spoon stirred in a teacup made a noticeable sound, and where in autumn one heard a crimped leaf strike the ground.

Happy, Happy, he sounded out her name to himself and—since the weather was so gorgeous and he felt a burst of sunshine in him—asked, "Do you think a name is a key to a person's personality?"

"Maybe," she said.

"I once thought about it," he said, thinking of Zoe and how he had once analyzed her name. "A name often shapes a person's way in life."

She looked up to the sky, thought about it. Maybe she'd find the answer written in the stars, if she could see the stars by daylight.

"Mmm," was her response.

"Do you like your name?" he tried again. If the conversation flagged now, all the magic that was created, the *spettacolo* of his monologue, would vanish into thin air. "Does it influence you?"

"Yes, I like it. But I don't know if it influences me. Maybe it does. Do you think it fits me?"

He nodded. "Yes. For sure."

"I can't think of any other name for myself," she said languidly, then at once seemed to rise from her lethargy. "I'd be furious with Brenda," she said, suddenly animated. "Bored to death if my name was Frances, or, ugh, Wendy."

She shifted her glance from his table to hers. His laughter made her beam.

"Why don't you bring your coffee over here?" she asked.

"Because I thought I'd invite you to join me. . . . But, okay, fine, that's what I'll do. Would you like another cup?"

"No, thanks. I'm finished. Got to get back to work soon."

"Work?" You mean you're not on vacation?"

"Nope."

"Do you work around here?"

"Uh-huh . . . not far."

And now they both breezed along on the skiff called Chit-Chat; skiff, though gondola would have been more fitting. But a gondola needs a gondolier, and who needs a third wheel on a two-person skiff, to mix the metaphor and add on weight? Now they talked about the weather, the city, the vaporetti, where they've been, what they've seen. He blessed the smallness of Venice that permitted a girl who had vanished on a vaporetto a couple of days earlier to reappear on the Piazza. Excited by her attentive gaze, he wondered if she were staying for the Festa del Redentore? What? she asked. You don't know what the Festa is? he asked, incredulous. Would she be staying another ten days? Of course, she said. I'm working here, remember? Of course I remember, he said. I just forgot. He told her about the Festa. But "told her" is a mammoth understatement. He sang a paean to its glories. You make it sound so interesting, she said, I can't wait to see it.

He studied her pretty face, couldn't take his eyes off her kissable lips. How many hours or days would it take for his lips to be on hers? She was young, he noticed. But those blue patches under her eyes made her seem older than twenty-two. He wouldn't ask straight out; it would look too avuncular. He learned it was best for the woman to volunteer her age herself. If he told his age, her response would come sooner or later. Anyway, he had his little secret way of telling how old they were, like rings on a tree, or teeth on a horse, for women always lied about their age. Especially women in their forties; that is, those who claimed they were in their forties. The fiftyers couldn't lie anymore. When they were younger, at the altar, their daddies gave them away. Now their necks did. The throat couldn't lie. Only the mouth. Actually, fingers and backs of hands told all. Cosmetic surgery could do lots, but not everything. Of course, with Happy none of these caveats were applicable.

She was a young chick, more or less.

"Have you been here often?" she asked.

Ah, here was an opportunity to tell her how old he was. He could use almost any word or turn of the conversation to get to age. Aged cheese, old ferry boats, milkweed, moonbeams, motherhood.

"I've come a few times," he said, not wanting to show off. "First time was when I graduated Dartmouth, just about, let's see, seventeen years ago."

She did some figuring. He thought she'd react somehow to the school, but that too passed her by.

"Then you must be thirty-eight."

"Thirty-nine," he said, shaving off eight years because he liked the ring of the thirties. Also he loved Jack Benny.

"You're thirty-nine?" she said.

"Surprised?"

"Yes."

"I celebrated my thirty-ninth birthday," he said carefully.

"How many years ago?"

He looked at her, wondering if the little witch had penetrated his disguise.

"Just kidding," she said. "I meant from now. You look so young."

He looked at his watch. "Am I keeping you?"

"It's okay. A few more minutes."

The waiter came. Tom told him in Italian that they were done.

"You speak Italian," Happy said admiringly.

He nodded. "I minored in it at Dartmouth."

"Do you use it in your work?"

"Only tangentially."

"What sort of work?" she asked.

By the warmth of her voice Tom could tell it wasn't just a polite question.

"Design," Tom said.

"Of women's clothing?" she said hopefully.

It was always that way. The minute he said design, they assumed it was women's clothing. God forbid it should be boxes or cars. Next would come the request for discounts. If not by the fourth exchange, surely by the seventh. Of course he didn't tell everyone he was a designer. Only those people with whom he had a chance encounter. Friends and kin knew he was a corporate speechwriter. And since you're a friend, now you know too.

No, Tom told her, it wasn't clothing. "I work with automobiles. We design the look that cars will have five-ten years down the, no pun intended, road." Then, suddenly, as if someone had slapped him in the face, he had a change of heart. Never mind the auto design bluff. He'd tell her the truth. Why fabricate? Why? Because, like ripe fruit, lies are out there, lurking, ripe, ready to be plucked. But no sense starting off with a lie, Tom felt, for one lie had a glutinous attachment to another. There was no escaping it. No wonder the Italian folk saying went: The truth is the best lie.

Happy stood. "Now I gotta go."

He stood too. "See you later? What time do you get off?"

"Let's see, tonight not till 9:30. Is that all right?"

"Sure. Super. Meet you here?"

She nodded.

"We'll walk around. I'll show you some spots I bet you haven't seen before."

"Like the ones on your shirt?" she said as she walked away, then threw over her shoulder, "What's 'tangentially'?"

At 9:25 he started looking for her.

At 9:35 he was restless. His skin tingled with kinetic energy, buzzing as though bees were nesting there. He sharpened his glance.

Ten minutes later he started walking around the table, always keeping his eye at one point, like a ballerina.

At 10 his heart started pounding. He counseled patience. Told his heart to stop, his skin to cease tingling. But it did no good. He still felt rotten. Stood up, he said to himself. Stood up, dammit. He started making larger and larger circles around the table, like a dog on a leash, always keeping an eye on the table. Why didn't I take her phone number? Even if he wanted to go to her place, even if he knew where it was, dammit, he didn't know the name of the pensione, wasn't sure he could retrace his steps. And what if he could, what if he went there and she came here and didn't find him? He was bound to this place, as if chained to it. What to do now? Why didn't he give her the name of his hotel? Why didn't he ask her last name, for goodness sake!?

He no longer bothered to look at his watch. Didn't want to give her the satisfaction. But the Bell Tower tolled the bells for him and he knew what time it was. How long does one wait? Is there a protocol for being stood up? Do you wait twenty minutes? Forty? An hour? And what if she shows up, apologetic, with a perfect excuse, a minute after he leaves? What then? How do you put Humpty Dumpty together again?

He drank one cup of coffee after another, but instead of calming him it made him more edgy. He cursed the wasted time, his stupidity in not making a backup plan. Why was that always a concern in his life—how long to wait for a girl who was late? Why did he have to see her on the vaporetto? But wait. He would have seen her anyway at Florian's a day later. There was no eluding destiny. But it just wasn't fair, getting a taste of her and then having her snatched away. It was as if a demon were dangling a golden apple in front of him and each time he went to take a bite—he jerked the apple away.

When he heard the gong strike eleven, he returned morosely to his dreary room. I don't like her any more, he vowed. Not interested in her. She doesn't deserve my attention, my longing, my fantasies and dreams. He looked in the mirror, too hurt and exhausted to make faces at himself. The visage he saw was a face already, one of his least imaginative concoctions. He returned to his bed and slammed his fists into the pillow, chanting, Dammit, dammit, dammit, why did I let her get away? I lost her, found her, lost her again, found her again. Now she's really lost. A three-time loser am I. Why do I let all the girls who mean something to me slip through my fingers?

He fell asleep with his clothes on, hoping that somehow she would find him and come to the hotel and ask the night clerk to wake him. So immured was he in fairy tales and make-believe, he actually considered this a possibility. He dreamt he rode a horse along a narrow sidewalk next to a canal. The horse kept slipping, finally throwing him into the water. A passing gondolier fished him out. Next, he finds himself sitting at Florian's with Happy. As Happy gets up to go to the bathroom, Zoe shows up, watching Happy leave. Zoe kissed him amicably on the cheek and cheerily stage whispered, "Who's she?" Tom finds himself tongue-tied. Finally, he manages to stammer hoarsely, "It's my half-sister." "Funny," Zoe says, "she's my half-sister too." "Which half?" he asks. "Dump her," Zoe says, a phrase he realizes that even in a dream Zoe would never use. "She's a kid... You're old enough to be her father." At this he woke. In the dark, in the absolute stillness of a Venice night, he realized he'd lost Happy. He wanted to go back to sleep and never wake again until she came, a Princess Charming, kissed his cold lips, and brought him back to life.

He got out of bed, looked out his window. The night was warm, warm and still. Nor sound, nor breeze. He looked down into the little gondoliers' canal on the side of the hotel. What to do tomorrow? he wondered.

He would go to that same table and sit there until she showed up. History would repeat itself. Destiny would get another chance. We'll turn the clock back and run the same scenario again. She'll come same time as yesterday, with an explanation. A good one, an honest one, which he'd accept, then she'd mouth, I'm sorry, with a melancholy smile. But if she doesn't show, if her third vanishing was her final one, it was a sign that he'd been mistaken again, was unable to judge a flighty character, a tease, a witch, a bitch who enjoyed leading a man on, and by the nose, only to dump him into the lagoon like a skittish horse.

Serves me right, he thought. I should be recalling Zoe, and here I am discomfited by a well-stacked blonde whose personality shifts. What one saw the second time wasn't what one saw the first. My punishment for not being faithful to Zoe.

7. The Meaning of Dreams

At 9:15 the next morning he sat at the café, reading *Il Veneziano*, gazing around him for signs of her, but trying not to be too obvious, trying to suppress his interest, trying not to show his agitation. But those kiss-me lips kept surfacing. Why had she been so friendly if she had a mind to dump him so quickly? Something was radically amiss. Could he have so misjudged her personality? What was wrong with him, acting like an adolescent? Act your age, Tommy. For goodness sake, you're forty-seven. That is, thirty-nine.

Just then a news item caught his eye that made him forget where he was. In Venice, yesterday, he read, a horse being led on a narrow walkway along a canal to the La Fenice Theatre slipped on a wet paving stone and pushed the groom into the water. Had Tom read this before and hence his dream? Or did some unconscious message send both his dream and the horse the same tidings? He put the paper down. No, I didn't read that. The words of my dream are being projected onto the newsprint and I'm reading back my own dream. He folded the paper and sipped some water to anchor himself. As he turned to look around, there she was again at the next table, smiling solicitously at him with a look that said, I was wondering how long it would take you to see me. Sitting calmly, as if she weren't the cause of an upheaval in him. As if it were yesterday or the day before all over again.

"How'd you get here?"

"I flew."

"How long you been here?"

"Six minutes. Watching you reading."

"Where were you last night?" he said, restraining his fury. He heard the tremor in his voice. "Why didn't you come? How'd you know I'd be here?"

"Weren't you here yesterday at this time? I had a hunch you'd be here." She stood, came up to him, took his hands. "I'm sorry. I'm so sorry. Their little girl got sick and I had to stay with her."

What a load of baloney, he thought. "What's wrong with her Mama?" he said.

"The parents hosted a wedding party. That's exactly why I was hired. For situations like that. I'm so sorry. I had no way of getting in touch with you."

"And I had all kinds of wicked thoughts about you stooding . . . standing me up. I was waiting and waiting. For hours! Riveted to this spot, figuring the minute I left, a minute later you'd show up."

"I'm sorry," she said softly. Those kissable lips, so kissably pink, no makeup, were pouting. "How long did you wait?"

"I'm still waiting."

"Oh my God! Please forgive me. You didn't go to bed. You waited for me here, on this metal chair, all night long."

He looked sullenly at her. Let her think what she thinks.

She sat herself on his lap and put her arms around him. "Sometimes something like this causes people to draw closer together, don't you think?"

"If you say so," he said. "And I couldn't contact you. I don't even know the name of your pensione."

"Grand Pensione Roma."

He laughed. "The fancier the name, I discovered, the smaller the hotel."

"I'm free now. . . . They gave me off a couple of hours, on account of last night."

"Did you tell them you had a date, that there's no way of contacting him, that you might lose him forever?"

"I told them I met this wonderful guy. . . . They felt so bad. But their daughter felt worse. . . .Come on! Are we going to sit here and mope?"

He eased her off his lap and jumped up. "You're right! Ready to see my Venice?"

"All the spots on your shirt I haven't seen before." She kissed his cheek. They pressed foreheads and looked into each other's eyes. "Yes," she whispered. She closed her eyes even before his lips touched hers. Then she dashed to her table and took something from the chair next to hers. A little packet wrapped in lavender tissue paper.

Shyly, she handed it to him.

Shyly, he took it. "Peace offering?" he said awkwardly.

"Why not?" Happy said.

He opened it, sensed what it was after he removed a few layers of the wrapping: a miniature lead gondola.

You know how many gondolas I have? he was about to say, but stopped himself. He also didn't tell her his definition of a gift: something you never want for yourself but don't mind getting for others.

"Thanks," he said. "It's beautiful. It's what I always wanted."

She picked it up and admired it.

"I got it because I dreamt last night me and you were in a gondola and it tipped over and you fell in."

She took a sip of water from his glass.

What kind of messages were being sent to him? he thought. That he was all wet? All he needed now was for Happy to knock his little gondola into the glass, like a magic act of transference. He watched her holding it, enjoying it, as if she had bought it more for herself than for him. She ran her fingers over it tenderly, erotically almost. He imagined her tongue gliding over it. Then, plunk, she either dropped it into the water or it slipped out of her fingers. Down it sank to the bottom of the glass. Little bubbles rose in the water. As if the gondola were a living thing giving up its last breath. He knew she would drop it. There was no doubt in his mind that her fingers would let it go. It depressed him, that upended gondola. Three times in the water.

Once in Happy's dream, once in his, once by Happy's clumsy fingers.

She plucked the little gondola out of the glass and waved it in the air to dry it.

"Is this a hint?"

"I didn't mean for it to drop," she said. "It just slipped in all by itself."

He wanted to say something about a Freudian slip, but changed his mind.

"You want to go for a gondola ride?" he said.

"You're not afraid to go after my dream?"

"I don't read dreams as omens. Come."

He took her by the hand and went to a gondolier's station away from the Piazza where the prices were lower.

In the gondola he asked her, "Ever been in a gondola before?"

"No. This is my first time."

"That's what they all say."

"And you?" Happy asked.

"I've been in a gondola before, but always alone. Never with a girl."

As they glided under a dark bridge, she kissed him, then as the bridge floated over their heads, she whispered, "What's 'tangentially'? You still didn't tell me."

He looked up to the bridge, thought he saw Zoe standing there. He knew she'd be here. That's why he came. I knew it, I knew it, he said to himself. I knew you'd be here, I just knew it, he rehearsed telling her. Zoe gave him a puzzled look, as if wondering what he's doing with that blonde in the gondola. When he looked again, Zoe had disappeared. She'll find me, he thought. But hopefully when I'm alone. I'll find her in one of the usual places. Just like I found Happy. People don't disappear in Venice.

8. *What He Does, What She Does, What They Did*

After the gondola ride he walked with her along the Riva degli Schiavoni.

"This, right here" —their backs to the Hotel Danieli—is where I first laid eyes on you, thinking that you'd vanished forever."

She smiled, but said nothing about noticing him.

"I have to make a correction," he admitted. "I was pulling your leg yesterday about design. In a way, I guess, I *am* in design. I design speeches. That's what I actually do—write speeches."

"Speeches? For whom?"

"Business executives. And occasionally I free-lance for politicians. But the . . . those, honest to God, I'm not allowed to reveal. That's part of the job. That I'm sworn to."

"Okay, I won't ask." A little teasing smile flittered, twinkled really, on her face, as if the smile belied the remark just made. What she meant was, I won't ask you just now, but you'll tell me in due time. You'll tell me all by yourself, you will.

"What about you?" Tom asked her.

"Nothing exciting."

"People always say that. Exciting is somehow always what the next guy does, never what one does oneself. So let's hear it. What you're doing."

"What I'm doing," Happy said in a soft, self-deprecating tone, "is slowly making my way through Europe. With stops to earn a little money. After I graduated . . ."

"College?"

"A community college, two years, you know, and then I worked a few years as a secretary for a small advertising firm in Albany and then . . ."

"Albany? Incredible! I go there often."

"You do? That's my home town. Did you ever eat in the restaurant near the capital building?"

"Well, there's lots of them there. Why do you ask?"

"My dad runs a little restaurant."

"Which one?"

"The one where all the politicians go. Rockefeller ate there. Cuomo too. My dad met them all. Did you hear of The Power

Lunch?"

"Sure. I ate there a number of times."

"My God! So you've been to Albany?"

"No. They faxed me the meals. . . . Of course I been there! How could I have eaten there and not been there?"

"Easy. You have no imagination. Could you have been there and not eaten there?"

"Of course."

"Then why not vice aversa?" Happy asked.

His impatient look said: Don't be absurd. "I may even have met your father. A short, broad-faced, gregarious man?"

Happy was nodding.

"Solidly built, with a small gray mustache?"

Smiling now.

"About sixty-two or sixty-three?"

Nodding vigorously.

"Very open, very welcoming, your dad. He was so nice. He took me back into his immaculate kitchen. All windows. He said something I'll never forget. He said, 'You see this light? The windows? I work with lots of light. It takes sunlight to grow food and I feel it takes sunlight, or at least lots of daylight, to cook food. I can't cook in the dark.'"

Happy smiled broadly. "No, that's not him."

Tom burst out laughing.

"That's our manager," Happy fairly shouted. "No, just teasing. Yes, that's him. . . . So, you met my father. . . . It's like, how can I put it?—destined?"

"Interesting . . . meeting a girl's father before the girl. Usually it's the reverse. . . . Want to sit down here for gelato?"

"No. Let's walk some more." She put her hand into his. They walked up a bridge. At the foot, he thought, I'm going to kiss her again. He led her to water. They watched the boats, then he turned her to him and kissed her.

"I interrupted you before. You were saying you worked for a small advertising firm."

"Yes. And then I decided it was time to do my thing."

"Let me do *my* thing." And he kissed her again, her lips, her mouth, her smile.

"Did you think of settling down?"

"You sound like my mother. . . . I got time." She laughed. Now she held his cheeks with the palms of her hands and pulled his face close to hers and kissed him, humming "Mmm" during the kiss. "Although my Mom doesn't think I have time. For her and her friends it's sort of embarrassing that a thirty-year-old daughter isn't married yet boy do you kiss good!"

Bingo! There it came. On its own. The age. Tom held her shoulders, looked warmly into her eyes.

"You? Thirty? Impossible! You look like a kid. I took you for twenty-one, twenty-two tops."

"Thanks, but like the . . ." She looked clearly at him with her light blue eyes, then hesitated as if searching for a metaphor, although the syntax seemed to mitigate against it. "But that's the age."

Tom looked at Happy's face, disguising the intensity of his scrutiny with a playful smile. He liked those little blue patches under her eyes, which even makeup could not hide. They seemed to glow deeper blue the more animated she became. If she's thirty, he figured, then her parents had her rather late.

"Did you say your father was sixty-three?" he asked.

"No, you did. Actually, he's sixty-five. He's going to retire soon."

"And do what?"

"Open a restaurant," she said and laughed.

"My m . . ." and she sneezed delicately—ptsee!—then pulled her right earlobe three times.

Tom looked at her quizzically.

"It's for good luck... My mom, who's part gypsy, taught me that. In fact, she taught me lots of exotic, unbelievable things."

"Tell me about them."

"Some other time, okay?"

He didn't press her.

"Having a job here must be wonderful! Being able to stay in Venice and even make some money. That I haven't been able to swing yet."

"Well, the money's not great—but at least I don't have to pay for basics. I work in a little off-beat family hotel where I have a tiny room and do odd jobs, like baby-sit, and teach their kid a little English. It's not too bad and it gives me a chance to spend some time here." She stopped, opened her eyes wide, and said, "I love this city. I mean, I lo-o-ove it." She stretched the word erotically. Tom half expected her to slowly run her tongue over her upper lip. "I'm crazy about this place. I wish I could stay here forever."

They turned into Via Garibaldi.

"Have you been on this street before?"

She said no.

"Few tourists know it. It's the widest street in Venice. Come."

They walked in silence a while, watching the Venetians talking and strolling on their street. Happy peeked into baby carriages and smiled at the mothers.

"What do you love about Venice?" he asked, expecting her to say its beauty, its uniqueness, its architecture, its history, its singularity, its city-as-a-work-of-art. But she said with a perfectly straight face:

"No traffic," and both of them burst out laughing at once.

"Come on! Really! And since when have you loved it?"

"Ever since I saw pictures of it," she said.

"Ditto for me. It seems that for most everyone the pictures precede. My dad showed me pictures of it when I was a kid. He told me that they had canals instead of streets, and in my child's imagination I pictured flooded streets, rivers running through avenues, and I couldn't imagine how people crossed the streets."

"So you must like Venice too?"

"Do trees have leaves? Do fish have scales?" He thought of running his tongue over his upper lip. "I lo-o-ove it."

"What do you love about it?" Happy asked. "And since when?"

Tom put a finger to his lips, as if considering the question.

"Its beauty," he said. "Its uniqueness, its architecture, its history, its spectacular singularity, its city-as-a-work-of-art. The entire panoptic of Piazza San Marco. Its quiet and its, let's see, above all, its lack of traffic." He didn't let her laugh too long and broke in with:

"I also like it because here I'm not a slave to the radio news. Back home it's part of my professional responsibility to listen to the news so often—you see, my speeches have to be timely—that on the hour I would hear the beep-beep-beep of the network news and, mark this!, the radio would be nowhere in sight."

She looked a bit puzzled listening to this, as if she couldn't quite grasp the surrealism of Tom listening to radios that weren't there. But her look of ambiguity soon faded into a fetching smile, which on a girl erases all doubts in the fella's mind about her ability to grasp the semi-palpable.

9. Happy's Will Power

When they passed the Danieli on their way back, Tom couldn't help thinking about how he and Zoe had gone in one day to take a look. At the Piazza, they sat on a stone abutment of the Basilica next to the Doge's palace, Tom telling Happy what he had told Zoe years and years ago.

"I tell you, I love sitting here. It's like sitting inside a poem. There is nothing, nothing in this world that can match this view. One of its glories is that it has remained, miraculously, the same over the centuries. Just look at it. This is the most harmonious square in the world. The world's largest work of art. When I'm looking at it, it's mine. It's real. It's here. It's what I've come for. But yet when I step into the calle away from the square—it immediately becomes a memory." Like Zoe has become. No, not become. She's not a memory, he thought. She's real. "I might as well be in Timbuktu."

What was he doing? Reciting a love poem to her? Or to Venice? How absurd it must seem to Happy to be hearing this. He muted his song and chanted to himself. Ruskin loved this place. Byron. Henry James did too. Who doesn't love this Venice? If one could embrace a city, I'd throw my arms around it and hug it to my chest. There was no feeling like returning to it, he thought. As soon as he set foot in Venice again, he smelled the familiar salt/fish tang of the canals. He loved the glint of the sun on the dark green water; he loved every curve of the bridges; the up and down walks, as if riding a series of prone parentheses, and sailing on the Grand Canal, pretending it was an inundated main street.

"You're, like, poetic. I love poetry."

"But I'm not a poet."

"You are. Anyone who says, It's like sitting inside a poem, is a poet."

"There's one more thing about Venice, important for me. Let's not forget it begins with a V. A strong, assertive letter that starts out at one point and branches in two directions without losing its base. Conversely, from two directions it arrows into one single point."

"You're funny," Happy said. "You have a mystic bend of mind."

"There's a touch of that in everyone, but it has to be tapped. Me, for instance, I like to zero in on letters. Everyone has strong letters in his life. V is mine. From Vermont, my home state, to Venice, my favorite place, the V has those directions that converge into one point, which is me."

And there's also Z, but he wouldn't tell Happy this. Z is etched into my life, he thought. Two V's sideways, sharing like Siamese twins a diagonal line, make one Z. From Vermont to Venice and Zoe. Z, the least letter used, but the one that most often sizzles in the lockbox of my mind.

He sang his song of love to Venice. But it was to Zoe, he knew, he was directing his song.

"I didn't come upon Zenice by myself. What am I saying, Zenice? I mean Venice. It was my dad who recommended it, or did I tell you this already?"

"No, you didn't. You said he showed you pictures and described it."

"He said, When—not if, but when—you go to Venice, you must first see it from a boat, like most visitors have throughout the ages. Not by train. And that's what I did. And I saw that magnificent panorama of the Doge's Palace and the Piazza floating out toward me like the architects intended. . . . I mentioned I've been here several times. But I tell you, I was here even before I was here. My dad's descriptions, works of art, Canaletto especially, and countless photographs."

"Is it a vacation this time too?"

"Yes. Plus an appointment I made some time ago, a meeting or two. Call it some unfinished business." He wondered if he said the last sentence out loud.

When they were parting, Tom didn't know whether to tell her that every single thin, lithe, small-waisted, curvy blonde he'd seen since that day she sailed away on the vaporetto reminded him of Happy. He looked for her everywhere he turned. Whichever girl he saw he hoped would be Happy. Wouldn't it sound overbearing if he told her this on the first day they met? No, he decided, and told her.

Happy gazed down modestly at her ankles, as if shy at hearing such an undeserved tribute. She merely mumbled "Ditto," then smiled up at him.

That ditto and that smile gave this guy who fell in love with every girl who was whisked away by subway cars or vaporetti such a high of bliss, he thought he was in heaven, or better, whisked to the top of the Bell Tower looking down at the Piazza.

"I remembered you too," Happy said. "I saw you standing at the pier looking at me, but disguising it by looking elsewhere."

"Oh, I did not. I looked straight at you. But your disguise was best of all. You didn't even look at me."

"But I did," she said. "I looked and saw. With a different type of seeing."

He considered that, but somewhere in his heart, he felt something amiss. Like an old photograph, he called back in his mind the image of Happy sailing away on the vaporetto, apparently disappearing from his life forever, her hands to her blonde hair to protect it from the wind. But wait, now her hair was brown, he told her. Yes, she admitted, she had had blonde hair (he adding the extra "had" as an act of pluperfect cortesia) the other day.

"And since then you dyed your hair brown."

"No," she said. "Not dyed."

"How then?" he wondered. "Some Jackson Pollock dripped brown paint on it? Or perhaps it was dusted with brown powder by an angel. Or maybe another process?"

"Uh-huh."

"Like pills," he joked.

"Like will power," she said. "Like wishing it." And she gave a cat-like smile. It reminded him of a picture he'd seen in a gallery the other day. It was a twelve- or fourteen-year-old girl, sitting at a window, stroking a cat, with a deep-eyed, gypsy-like, feline smile, all lips, no teeth, her face radiating cattiness and mystery.

"Gotta go," she said. "Back to work." She stood on tiptoe and whispered into his ear. "I got a secret to tell you."

The girl's in love with me already crossed his mind.

"I'm all ears."

She put her lips to Tom's ears. "What's 'panoptic', and what's 'gregarious', and why do you use such big vocabulary words?"

But before he a chance to answer, she gave him a delightful smile and bounded away.

Happy went back to work; he went to the American Express office. Hanging around for a few minutes, looking at some bulletins, hoping. Hoping for what? A return of the past. He attempted that back home one day, inspecting an old passport photo of himself taken before his first European journey, trying to remember what he looked like when he met Zoe. To see the face she saw. Saw himself staring into the camera with big bright eyes and a slightly mocking look that said, I'm too good for passport photographs. The Mona Lisa tease of his eyes made the pursed lips seem smug. I'm young, bright, successful, he seemed to say. I can pass through any port without documentation.

10. The Fickle Color of Her Hair

He saw Happy every day. Sometimes twice a day, whenever she had off. Sometimes he would walk her back to her pensione, sometimes she insisted on going alone. Once, when the light was right, the sunlight on it, he saw an old brass plaque on a private villa at the edge of a canal:

Here resided Count Moise Guido Veneziano-Tedesco
(1840-1930)
Senator and Physician to all Venetians
Honorary First Citizen of Venice

"My God," Tom told her, "this is incredible."

"Why, what's up?"

"I went to school—I took my junior year at Columbia—with a guy named Guido Veneziano-Tedesco, who came from Venice. He later became photography editor at the *Long Island Post*. This must be his grandfather. What a coincidence! It's like me meeting you."

"There are no coincidences," Happy declared. "Everything is prearranged."

The first Sunday they spent the entire day together. He showed her his Venice, the Venice she never would have known. But he couldn't go to her place; she couldn't even show him her room, she said. The owners forbade it. That was one of the conditions of employment: no visitors, male or female. But she came to his little hotel, in one of the calles near Piazza San Marco, right off one of the small canals. At night he took her dancing. She told him, "You dance so beautifully," and he said, "You follow beautifully." Then, after what he considered a brilliant comic pause, he added, "You'd make a great fascist."

She leaned her head against his chest and laughed, but he couldn't be sure she fully understood the resonance. What he did remember was a look she gave him the next day, a look that could only come in public, when other eyes were around, never in private, for a look like that had a radiance only in the outside world. It sent a secret message when others were around. They were sitting in a café and Tom was engaged in a long conversation with the waiter. Happy stared admiringly at him and he turned and caught the warmth of her glance. But then came Zoe again. She lurked not far off. She montaged herself into every picture. Now he thought of the light that had come from Zoe's eyes years ago, a radiance he had never forgotten. Where had they sat? Probably in one of these cafés, because he purposely chose cafés where he and Zoe had been. Yes, this must be the place. How long they had gazed at each other he could not tell. Perhaps because such moments come only once and not again, they last longer in later recall than in reality. He couldn't describe the look in words; couldn't even imitate the incandescence of Zoe's eyes. Were he an artist, he might have been able to splash a rainbow on canvas to create an analogue to the light in Zoe's eyes; a composer—perhaps to sing a song without words to recreate it. Words just didn't have the power to reconstruct the mystery of eyelight.

He looked at Happy.

"Your eyes are glowing," she said.

"For you," he said.

Her eyes had a warmth, like Zoe's. But they couldn't match the real thing.

Happy gazed into his eyes. He let his eyes relax. She took his hand. "Let's exchange stories," she said. "I'll tell you about Albany, you tell me about Vermont... You know, it's so close, but you know I've never been there."

"Ladies first," he said.

"I'll talk about my mom. I love talking about her. She's unlike any other mom you've ever known. . . . She's half gypsy, you know. . . . Listen. . . . My development was sort of screwy. I developed only one breast, the left one. The right one just wasn't there. So I put a sock in my bra to even it out and then two more socks to make them look bigger, until one morning my mother caught me and pulled the socks away. God was slow, she said, but he'll make up for it in due time without your help."

"Well, he sure did make up for it," Tom said, looking down at her chest. "You sure don't need socks now."

She looked down too. Her eyes rolled from left to right. "I guess not."

"Now you need anti-socks, so other men shouldn't stare. Or flashing earmuffs to divert their attention."

"My mother also told me not to sleep on my back, but I didn't know why she said that until one summer night I lay in bed, on my back, and heard the wind blowing and the trees rustling, but there weren't any trees where I lived and I saw the devil's face on the ceiling coming closer, dropping closer and closer to me. I prayed and turned and hid under the pillow and my prayers made the face go back further and further away."

"It was headlights from a car, and the guilt from sleeping on your back made you susceptible to being 'punished,'" Tom explained.

"Maybe. But then it was real."

"Do you know why your mother told you not to sleep on your back?"

"Not then," she laughed. "But now I know why. Good girls don't lie on their backs."

"Right," he said. "*Guys* lie on their backs and the good girls sit on them. And then *they* lie about it. On their backs. Sitting down and standing up."

She smiled and fingered her hair, drawing his attention to it.

Her hair was blonde again, he finally noticed.

"What's with the hair? Colored it again? Or," he gave a skeptical little smile, "is it will power again?"

"It *is* will power. I wasn't joking. It's a special strength." She discovered it by accident, she said. Only it wasn't such an accident, because her half gypsy mother had laid hands on her and blessed her with a special power. "Anyway," she continued, "once I was laying in a lukewarm tub. There was no hot water. I closed my eyes and imagined that I actually felt warmer."

"Your will power actually made the water warmer?"

"Maybe yes. Maybe no. I didn't have a thermometer. All I know is that what I wished came about. I was comfortable. I had a hot bath."

"That sounds like some power you have. Do you have any weaknesses?"

"Yes."

"What?"

"If I say it, I'll lose my power."

"Like Samson with the hair?"

She didn't say. Maybe she didn't know about Samson with the

hair.

"Then what's your power?"

"I tell the truth."

"Always?"

"Yes. Except when I lie."

"How often do you lie?"

"Not as often as I should, but less than others expect."

"And the rest of the time you tell the truth?"

"Even more than that."

"That's a contradiction."

"Only when I'm caught."

11. Who Fills His Days, Who Fills His Thoughts

Yes, there was Happy to fill his days and some hours of the night. Yet sometimes he had the feeling that Zoe's arms were around him, not because Happy reminded him of Zoe but because Happy's warmth was like Zoe's. Maybe it was the way she snuggled up to him in bed and snoozed after making love. But despite Happy's love of sex no girl's orgasm could compare to Zoe's. When Zoe came, she felt it, in her words, from the back of the throat to the tip of her nose, from the top of her head to the tips of her toes. And their personalities were eons apart. Zoe's self-effacement was like a skin; Happy, like her name, wore her confidence like a halo. Yards away you sensed its light.

Say it in twenty-five words or less, Tom: Happy filled his days; Zoe filled his thoughts.

And if Happy sensed this, like a cork she bobbed into view, seeking attention.

"Do you miss me?" Happy asked.

"You're here now."

"When I'm away, I mean."

"Ask me then."

She laughed but made a face when the words sank in.

"I have no time to miss you," he tried to explain. "I see you all the time."

"I mean when I leave you."

"Then I can't wait for you to come back."

"So you do miss me."

"I didn't say that. I don't miss you so much when you're away as I do when you're here and thinking of when you won't be here. Understand?"

"No."

"Neither do I. Missing is very personal. Actually, non-transferable. Truth is, I don't miss anyone—except myself. But only when I'm away."

"Miss me," Happy insisted. "I know you're just saying that because you're uncomfortable telling me how much you miss me. I know you're shy. So don't tell me. You don't have to tell me. Just feel it. Miss me. Miss me. Miss me when I'm here and miss me when I'm away. . . . Do you hear me?"

A tough, determined girl was Happy. She stood her ground. Not self-effacing, shy and timid, timid and pavid like Zoe. He liked that, but didn't like it. Liked it for her pride of self; didn't because she was too influenced by the nether elements of pop culture; ground level, so to speak. He soon discovered that she knew the latest filthy expressions, had a handle on perverse sex—mickeys was her favorite —though she claimed she never saw things like mickeys, much less experienced them. Still, she knew about them. Could spend evenings watching porno flicks. Where she learned these things she didn't tell, was evasive. You know, you hear it, she said, like it's around you. In the office, in the gym, in school, in the cafeteria. You know, girl talk. You keep your ears open, you hear, you get to know. Mickeys, he sniffed. Mickeys, like in Mickey Mouse, don't you know, she offered. Where they put, she taught him, a baby mouse up a girl's pussy and watch her squirm with delight? How about horror? he suggested. She couldn't say—as the little critter makes its way up, or down, the paradisiacal channel. But why a mouse would want to scurry up that dark passage he could never fathom. But she told him she'd heard some girls love it. Resist at first, then love that soft furry thing moving up and down. How does it get out? Tom wanted to know. There's no room in there for a K turn. She hadn't the foggiest notion. Maybe, he suggested, they tied a string to its tail to pull it out. And what would happen if it dropped dead up there? Or fainted from the smell? She couldn't tell tall tales from truth, poor kid. The whole thing had an apocryphal ring to it.

Then, seeing how peeved he was at this, she began talking about her parents. Her dad and his little restaurant. He was a likable, run-of-the-mill sort of guy, Tom knew. But her mother, to hear her tell it, though half gypsy, retained more than her 50% share of those genes. She loved superstition, amulets, fortune telling, cards, folk magic, wax drippings, the works. It was only later, when Tom returned to the subject of her mom, that Happy told him that three days a week her mother had a little hole-in-the-wall storefront in a poorer section of town that once used to be a Jewish neighborhood, but with the Jews gone, all kinds of ethnics had come in, and there she ran a little fortunetelling, hocus-pocus atelier, making the Puerto Ricans, Dominicans and Senegalese feel good. It was this, along with Happy's knowledge of kinky sex, that gave him edgy, somewhat negative feelings. Still, he appreciated her bounce, her cheer, her joy, while trying to assess and digest her roughly honed persona. She was breaking out of low class, he knew, breaking out of the chrysalis, but was still not a butterfly.

Since she hadn't read a book, certainly not a good book, in years (Zoe, he remembered, devoured books, good ones too, by the dozen), he loved to tease her.

"Did you ever hear of the Danish writer, Borges?"

"Yes."

"What did you read by her?"

"I forget."

"No kidding! Wow!" he shouted. "'I Forget' happens to be one of her better known stories. Funny you should mention that one, it's my personal favorite. Remember how the hero locks his wife who is very sexy but stupid and illiterate as they come into a room and then forgets and goes on a three-day business trip? It's the first in her great collection, *The Minotaur Out of the Maze; or, Metaphysics Mimics Magic*. Critics don't know whether to praise her inter-textual sexuality, her intersexual self-reflectivity, or her pre-mythic, post-colonial multiorgasmic polyculturism."

On the other hand, what she didn't know about books she knew about people. Namely, him. Her eyes giggy-goggled about in her head re world culture, but they zoomed into focus where he was concerned.

She knew what she was about, not a snowflake of Zoe-like naiveté on her. She had a sharp eye, that one. For instance, his ears. (No wonder she gave a little smirk and cocked her head and raised her eyebrows the other day when he said, "I'm all ears.") Like his father and grandfather, Tom had long, lopey ears, which nothing, not hats, not hairdos, could disguise. But of all the girls he had known, none, including Zoe, had ever mentioned his ears to him. But Happy said, straight out and brightly, "I once saw a biography of Bing Crosby on tv. Did you know they used to tape his ears back in films? Did you ever think of doing that with yours?" "Never, why?" he said innocently. "Because," said Honest Miss Muffet, "they stick out and they're also too long." He told her, "It's a sign of royalty. Prince Charles also has big ears. We're descended from the Windsors. And what's more, they don't make invisible tape any more." On the other hand, no one else, including Zoe, ever noticed that soft blond baby fuzz curled like lashes on his upper cheeks; and no one but Happy, who scrutinized him with a magnifying glass in order to improve him and who, while inspecting his ears critically, praised the golden peach fuzz on them.

Yes, an eagle eye had she. A hair on the tip of your ears, she'd call it to your attention. A bit of scraggle left unshaven on the neck beneath the chin—the back of her hand would rub the skin in silent critical review. Two tiny hairs asquiggle on an eyebrow, out she'd point it to you with a little smile of triumph. No. Than a smile, more a smirk, the little witch.

Zoe was more placid, her head in the clouds. He couldn't imagine Zoe saying, Your socks don't match your pants. Why don't you shine your shoes?

And Happy had a tongue to match. When he told her what he had told Zoe years back about rural life and that the smells of earth and the stable clung to him, Happy pursed her lips like a naughty girl about to be impudent and said, "And they still do."

But what was the most annoying was her handle on the relationship. By her questions it was she who held the oar to the gondola.

What's gonna be? she asked him close to Festa day, not wanting to know about the world's future, that's fer sure.

Otherwise, she didn't talk much. Certainly not about books or art, politics or music. Other women yackety-yakked constantly. Not Happy. She was annoyingly quiet. Was she intimidated by him? Did he muffle her natural prolix? He laughed. Had he used that word with her, she'd've thought it was an over-the-counter medication, or some new-fangled contraceptive. Maybe it was because she was younger. They didn't dwell on that, but it wasn't far from his thoughts. In her mind he was nine years older, but he knew he was seventeen years older, a little fib so as not to drive her away and not prompt the classic cliché, You're almost old enough to be my father. But she never mentioned the nine years, even said at the outset that he looked younger than thirty-nine. Maybe the old Vermont truism that bachelors always looked younger held true. Indeed, he remembered the Wharton brothers, Dick and Bill, a couple of old bachelor farmers, in their upper seventies who had smooth, young, even virginal faces. Bachelorhood kept them young. They looked like they were in their early fifties. So surely it held for him too— aging bachelor that he was—looking much younger than his forty-seven years, able to pass himself off as thirty-nine. Even younger, had he wanted to. But even if she was younger, she could have asked other questions besides, What's gonna be? As if she were addressing some fortune-teller, some gypsy who would look into a crystal ball and tell her what song tomorrow's bird would sing.

But he didn't tell her what's gonna be. He didn't even know what's gonna be with himself, much less others. He didn't know what shape his life would take one week from now. He'd take it one day at a time, until the Festa del Redentore and a couple of days beyond that, when his stay in Venice would end, and real life— writing speeches—would resume. How could he know what's going to be with him, if he didn't know what's gonna be with the world? Once, long ago, as a child, he had worried about it. He remembers being ill, in his parents' bed, some kind of fever. He closed his eyes, concentrating hard, and tried to imagine what the world was like before the world was created. It was like trying to imagine himself not there. That globe of emptiness so vast it gave him a headache and elevated his temperature. He felt a hard pressure at the tip of his skull that vanished only when he opened his eyes and left the uncreated world and returned to his parents' bed. What the world would be like if there were no world was a thought that had plagued him for years.

Plagued him for years, plagued him for years. The words rose like a tide, each larger than the other until he was able to walk between them, swing around the pole of the "i" and slide down the crook of the "y" There was something else that had plagued Thomas Manning for years.

In the Vermont countryside, he would think of Venice, the masterpiece of man. And in the heart of Venice, watching the picture-book gondolier pushing his gondola, he would suddenly long for the greenery and open spaces of the Vermont hills. The heart always longs for elsewhere. What was it that drew him to Venice? Why did he love it so much? Because it was a testament to man? If the beauty of the forests and mountains, meadows and falls, were made by God, then the beauty of Venice was that it was all shaped by man. Man took that bit of land by the sea and carved canals, built bridges, planned San Marco, erected towers, and fashioned palaces and churches to dazzle the eye.

And then the voice within him, fighting sinew and steel, paper and skin, pecking like a chick's tiny beak at the shell until it saw the real light of the world, then the voice finally emerged from its fist-like incarceration.

Lies! All lies! Lies and hypocrisy!

Why don't you tell the truth, Thomas Manning?

Did you ever love Venice as much as you love it now?

And hasn't your love of the city increased since you first saw it twenty-five years ago? Loving it more with every yearly visit?

Raise your right hand and tell us and the gentlemen of the jury!

That there's only one reason—one, and only one—why you now adore Venice so much.

Zoe.

Her image, spread like a fine haze over the city, makes you seek out each calle and café, every corner and bridge, seeing if you can find her traces, sniffing for her smell, listening for her footsteps. Here we walked. Through these canals we rode the gondola. In this gelateria we ate gelato (raspberry, her; nucciola, me) for the first time. Here we heard a concert. The tinkle of a spoon in a glass was recalled as music from Zoe's time. Memory of Zoe drove the vaporetti around the S-curve of the Grand Canal.

And since he was confessing, he had to admit that he was also drawn to Venice for expiation. Again, Zoe. Zoe, once more. Every time he came to Venice he hoped maybe Zoe would be here— perhaps like moths they would both be drawn to its incandescence— and he could tell her he was sorry, sorry from the bottom of a pained heart, that he had abandoned her.

MIDDLE

1.Tasting Life More Than Once

By now he had Venice in his grasp. Venice from the roofs, the red tiles that cover the city, that roseate layer between pavement and sky; Venice from the air, the empty Piazza at dawn; Venice from the sea, the two-toned warning cry "Oi-eee!" of the gondoliers as they rounded corners. Oh, that musical splash in the profound stillness!

He remembered telling Zoe that the gondola was *la piu bella cosa che Dio gabio fato*—then translating it, of course: the nicest thing that God ever made. He told her the legend of the gondola. Its sickle shape comes from a new moon that once plunged into the Venetian lagoon. And because it was a heavenly body, he told Zoe, all the boats on the canal, big and small, live in harmony, in good rhythm with each other, like lovers.

And the light. Venice had a light of its own. People claimed that Greece had perfect light. But Venice had super perfect light. Every photo he'd taken of the city showed the crisp, translucent light. Light letting light through, the pristine meaning of "trans" and "lucent."

But he knew that all these thoughts of Venice were other-speaking for the real reality; his thoughts, though true, were masks, metaphors. It was not Venice he had in his grasp; it was Happy. He saw her wherever he went, up in the palaces with views of the roofs, on the water, in the gondola, at the cafés, everywhere it was Happy, Happy, Happy, he assured himself. But yet, in the secret symbolism of his thoughts, in the dreams that metaphors had, there was something else, as impalpable as light, eluding his grasp: Zoe. She was the light within him that would not darken. Because of her light he was able to see Happy.

This Zoe, this Zoe from so long ago, this Zoe like a dybbuk invaded him. Every time he left Happy, instead of enjoying the afterglow of her presence, the first person who scudded into his mind, like a yellow sailboat windblown on an ultramarine sea, or descending from the sky on a corn-yellow umbrella from the Rockefeller Center café, was Zoe. How could he enjoy Happy if Zoe crouched in back of his skull, and how could he enjoy the memory of Zoe, if Happy superimposed her image over Zoe's like a younger competitor?

Remembering was delicious. Remembering let him taste life twice. But the only trouble with remembering was—you can't forget. No matter how distant the past, memory compressed time and made it seem like yesterday. And sometimes you wanted to forget about yesterday. But the more you wanted to forget about yesterday the more it seemed like today. For ill or good he had a genius for memory. Events came back to him with eidetic precision as if they were happening again. Maybe he was the only man in the world who could taste life twice, a memory ruminant who could replay selected events again and taste them on the back of his tongue, savor the aroma of their delectable perfume. Or their taste of bitter gall.

2. The Atom that Defied Newton

He couldn't help it: Venice and Zoe, Zoe and Venice. In the middle of Piazza San Marco, the sounds of the café orchestra sent him across the sea and he stands at Rockefeller Center with Zoe by the balustrade of the skating rink listening to the café orchestra below the bright corn-yellow umbrellas that have trapped the ochre sun on the day he said *au revoir* to Zoe. At times he seemed to ride in two time zones under a cloud-frazzled sickle moon that would soon plunge into the water and transform its luminescence into a gondola that would take him and Zoe into hidden canals where, once they glided under a bridge, the gondolier kneeling in the prow, Tom would kiss her and he'd see Happy upside down bending over the bridge looking at him, watching him, not letting him out of her sight. On the two gondolas that were one, the now with Happy moving leisurely along, the years back with Zoe, zooming like a hydrofoil. The illogic of riding two gondolas at the same time at different speeds did not upset his equilibrium. But the sudden jolt of realizing with whom he really was unsettled him. His few days with Zoe years ago were so compressed in his memory, in depth like a hologram, that some of his activities with Happy, like strolling in off-beat Venice or exploring the quiet island of Giudecca, fused in his mind with the fun days with Zoe. Was it with Zoe or Happy that he had done this or that? On occasion, he had to backtrack and shake his head free of cobwebs that tangled his memories to realize that it was Happy he was with. This mix-up of reality and fantasy had happened before, but in a different way. Not girls, but an over-the-counter medication. Soon after swallowing the pill, letters were magically changing as he read. Dots rolled off i's and j's and fused like globs of mercury. Some words became invisible. He was unable to stop paragraphs repeating. Pages turned on their own accord. The author's name atop the page—he knew it was Hawthorne—kept appearing as Hawkins. During the hallucinatory stage, he wrote down "Hawkins" to remind himself of what was happening, but when the medication wore off he saw that the word he'd written was "Hawthorne". He recalled that eerie feeling when he thought of this Zoe/Happy shapeshifting, and wondered if perhaps she too thought he was someone else.

Seeing Zoe before his eyes surprised him at first and, on occasion, made him uncomfortable. He felt he was being unfaithful to both of them. But on the other hand, why feel bad? Why make a choice? Perhaps this threesome was a magical hint to him. After all, three was a magic number and the triangle an engineering emblem for sturdiness and strength. A classical threesome was mind, body and soul; hope faith and charity. So why choose? Especially since scientists had recently made a physics breakthrough, turning one of the bedrock laws of nature, one of the canons of Newton's laws, upside down: a beryllium atom was shown to be in two places at the same time. For Tom the implications were enormous; his desires were given a gargantuan boost. If an atom could defy one of the basic laws of physics, man was next. Which meant that he would be able to be with both Happy and Zoe at the same time. The other implication, for transmission of messages and electronic banking, didn't concern him. At any other time he would have been thrilled by the reversal of time as he was by the mysteries of space, but now even hearing that an extension of the atom discovery was that messages could be received even before they were sent did not excite him.

When he told Happy this, he was disappointed that it gave her no intellectual high, no cerebral spasm of ecstasy. She had a practical turn of mind, did Happy.

"Well, what does it mean, this one atom in two different places?"

"It means that what we thought of as the normal order of the world isn't that normal. Basic laws of physics are being suspended, uprooted, overturned."

"I can repeal those laws too. But let's make it practical. I'm not too good at abstract. How does it relate to you and me?"

"Simple. I'll give you an example. Normally, a person thinks something, says it, the other person hears it. But in this new order, it means you can hear me saying I love you before I even say it."

"Hey!" She jumped up and down and smiled and clapped her hands. "Did you hear yourself saying what you just said?"

"No."

"But I just heard it."

"That just proves my point. You heard it first."

"You said you loved me."

"I did?"

"Yes. You said it means you can hear me saying I love you even before I say it. . . . Oops!" She put her hand over her mouth. "I meant, *you* said I could hear *you* saying you love *me* before you said it."

"It's all theoretical. I meant that a *person* could tell someone else I love you, etc. before he even utters it."

She put her arms around him.

But even with her arms around him, Tommy couldn't get that atom out of his skull. If a person could be in two places at the same time, time had to stand still, even be reversed. If time could be reversed, then past events could be replayed. If so, he had a second chance. But even second chances and time reversal probably had their own laws. There wasn't total anarchy out there. Like Einstein said, God doesn't play dice with the universe with his one hand tied behind his back.

For instance, how may times could a past be replayed? After all, it wasn't a cassette tape. And how many choices does one have? Three? Like wishes in a fairy tale? Which event would he choose? With path to take? How could he right the wrong? The atom in two places concurrently opened the doors for him that he never dreamt could be opened. Rather, re-opened. Who said there wasn't a second chance in life? Scientists had demonstrated that the fantasies of science fiction were real. With the crumbling of the sacred laws of physics, science had given him an opportunity to rebuild himself. Humpty Dumpty *could* be put together again. But one would hope that in the process the remark that an old girl friend had made after a day of hectic shopping would not prove to be true: In the process of putting yourself together you fall apart.

But beryllium here, beryllium there, meanwhile he savored the pleasure of memory and accepted the shock of disappointment. Still, he tried to leap off those oarless gondolas that yoked past and present.

At times he felt that that slow gondola with Happy aboard had disappeared below the horizon and now he could focus on Zoe and persuade himself that he had come to Venice only for Zoe—to renew old memories. Isn't that so? he asked himself as he made faces in the mirror, wondering if one of them could serve as a mask on Festa night. Or was perhaps his real face his mask?

Good memories were so hard to come by, like the perfect pizza, so how could he just brush off thoughts of Zoe, even though Happy was more real. He still couldn't forget his last meeting with Zoe at Rockefeller Center. Though it had taken place years ago, he could still describe every turn of the conversation, every gesture, every hue of her now porcelain, now russet, powder-flecked face and her modest-seeming blouse and skirt. So kill me! he argued with his unseen accuser. What am I going to do? Rip out my mind? She's there because she's there. If she hadn't been at Amexco, bending down to pick up her things with me about to approach, I wouldn't be thinking about her.

Zoe was everywhere he looked: the Doge's Palace, the Piazza, in the music at every concert. He could have cried and at times he did—people around him assuming he was touched by the music—when hearing Vivaldi at one of the churches, and remembering how Zoe had sat next to him looking at him with her lamb eyes full of love, could have cried how they split up—

Split up?

Okay, abandoned her—

wishing at times that he had kept her, had her with him, had had a normal life with her, and wondering why he hadn't taken her as his own when everything seemed all right, just right, with them.

Everything he did in Venice made Zoe come to mind. He sees a group of Japanese tourists—again Zoe. Because he'd once told her a tall tale about raising his umbrella in a crowd of Japanese tourists crossing a bridge and watching them follow him like the Pied Piper as he turned into a calle. And if she didn't believe him, here it is, this calle over here, just past the Hotel Danieli.

He even saw Zoe in Happy's face. What next? he wondered. Will he see his own there too?

Was it wishful thinking he felt when he pressed his face to Happy's, or was it some magical transference, the lookalike cells jumping from one collagen to another?

Did he start it, or was it Happy who first declared:

"We look alike."

But he said nothing.

Maybe, he thought, she was saying it to increase the conjunction between them.

Hearing his silence, she presses her face to his by the mirror and said happily:

"Look!"

In the glass he saw it, or thought he saw it, for mirrors sometimes see better than the eye. She did look like him, so much so it was like gazing into a mirror, with a sex change. They had the same arched brows, that long line down the side of their cheeks, the same pouting lips. Or was she unconsciously imitating him? The next day they pressed their faces so tightly together before a small mirror that both halves of their cheeks looked like one.

"Siamese," one of them said, but Tommy forgot who.

"There are just so many facial types, it's a miracle more of us don't look like one another," he said. "It doesn't surprise me any more when I see someone who looks like me, or resembles someone else I know. I expect it. In fact, I'm puzzled when I meet someone who *doesn't* remind me of someone else."

"But still, I mean, isn't it, like, amazing?" Happy said excitedly. "How much we look like each other?"

"Except I have dark hair and you're a blonde."

"We look like each other," she insisted. "We look like each other." And to prove her point, by the end of their conversation her hair was brown again. But he didn't notice the change.

"Take the 'look' out of the sentence and you'll have a perfect thought."

That she didn't notice. The verbal gymnastic was too much for her.

But maybe they overdid it, got carried away, with looking alike. From both their desires to look alike—well, hers more than his; to share something beyond themselves—came the veil over their vision that made them believe it, much like a couple that wants to like each other jumps at points in common. Hey, both of us have been to Acapulco; hey, both of us like operas, popcorn, and broccoli, and we both hate guns, money grubbers and rubber gloves. So maybe their faces weren't really that close; perhaps they didn't look like each other at all but each saw the other through the other's borrowed eyes—i.e., the glances they exchanged a week or was it a year ago at the Café Florian on Piazza San Marco.

On the other hand, like he told her, looking alike was a cinch. After all, God can make just so many faces. Years back, Tom had dropped off a girl friend on the East Side of New York and drove across town, through Central Park, to the West Side, and there on West 67th Street, in mid-block, there she was, same long black hair, glasses on her nose, roundish face. Even built the same way. He wanted to stop, have a look, talk to her, ask her how she had made her way to the West Side so quickly, but the traffic was heavy behind him, and even for the two seconds he slowed down, behind him horns blared and honked and he had to move ahead.

"Look, I'm going to teach you to make faces in the mirror, and then when we're good enough we can make faces at each other, and we'll see who laughs first. But don't get too used to yourself on the mirror or you'll think of your image as the real person and the real you as just a reflection. So remember, left is right and right is left; otherwise you remain in the mirror forever."

"Doesn't frighten me," she said at once. "If that happens, I have a magic formula that can undo it."

Looking alike was one thing; it was almost credible. But sharing dreams was something from la-la-land. He first discovered this when he told Happy the beginning of a dream he had. At once she interrupted: That's my dream! (He didn't believe her. How could he? People share beds, baths, bagels, maybe even thoughts. But dreams?) And promptly finished the dream for him.

The next time this happens, if such an oddball thing *can* happen again, he told her, let's both write down the dream, to ensure that neither party is faking. The next time they both dreamed that he was giving a lecture to a group on three-party sex, had a bunkbed onstage and asked for two volunteers. (In his dream the two volunteers were girls; in hers, two guys.) Must be your influence, he said, waking up for the first time to the long dormant suspicion buzzing around in his head like an insistent gnat—bzz, bzz, magic formula for reversing being stuck in a mirror; bzz, bzz, changing your hair color; bzz, bzz, warming bath water by will—that Happy was, if not a witch, then a very strong sympathizer, for I never usually have dreams like that. You wrap yourself, entwine yourself around me and put that into my soul, he told her, with genial complaint. Do you dream like that all the time? Constantly, she said, but it's only a dream. You've never done anything like that? he asked. No, never.

He told her it was bewitching. It's your doings, these dreams.

She smiled ambiguously, but seemed pleased having him think it was her doing.

Yes, they had the same dreams, but there was one dream that was his alone (or was it? for if she had imposed it on him, then it wasn't his alone; or maybe she had it too, in her version, but didn't tell him.) What he didn't tell her was that he also dreamt that she was being screwed by his friend and he asked her, Was it good? And she said, Yes, he was very gentle, very slow, sensitive, caring. Did he eat you? And in his dream, Happy said brightly, "Yes, he gobbled me up till there was nothing left of me and that was good too," and he had this awful feeling of jealousy in his gut, but yet he felt good that she didn't leave him and that it was just a dream. In his dream it didn't bother him that much, because in his dream he announced loudly—but not loud enough to wake him up—that it was only a dream.

3. Any Secrets?

The days passed, some slowly like Happy's gondola, some quickly, like Zoe's, moving inexorably to the Festa that Tom looked forward to. Maybe even with some trepidation. For the coming of the Festa would mean the end of the vacation. And then what would he do, what with thoughts of Zoe in his heart, with himself and with Happy, this ghostly triangle of his own creation?

What's gonna be? Happy had asked him. About his inner self she never even dreamt of asking. Never probed why at thirty-nine this good-looking, self-confident, apparently successful guy hadn't married, or if he was married, where was his wife? And how did he look at himself in the mirror when she wasn't there looking with him? Questions like that were foreign to her. But one question did come up one evening after he had pulled her leg with some absurd remark like:

"Wouldn't it be funny if one day we wake up and the first news bulletin we hear says that new scientific research shows that smoking is good for you, breathing trucks' black diesel fumes prompts oxygenation of your blood, food dyes prevent strokes, massive doses of animal fat rejuvenate the heart muscles, pesticides strengthen nerve endings, nitrites grow new hair, preservatives enhance vision, blubber in pot bellies aids digestion, and exercise leads to kidney collapse?"

Instead of replying, the little airhead suddenly asked, "Do you have any secrets?"

Tom thought for a moment, eyes up, brows knotted in thinking position. But he wasn't thinking. He was shocked at the sharp angle of the question, the newness of it, its sheer gall. As if a new Happy, with a different brain and set of attitudes stood before him. That's why he posed a thinking pose, made her believe he was ruminating, when he was actually absorbing the shock of her probing question.

"No." Paused. "At least none that I can reveal."

She smiled at the irony of his remark, just as he could have laughed at the oxymoronic nature of her question.

"You're funny," she said.

"Well, at least that's no secret."

But then he realized she wasn't an airhead at all. She was what he suspected her of being: a witch. The little witch had again penetrated his thoughts. He *had* a secret but he wasn't about to share it with her, or with anyone. Happy had a secret too. It was perfectly obvious. She dreamed his dreams, could almost read his thoughts, changed the color of her hair, and warmed bath water just by concentration. Her mama was half gypsy. And Happy had either learned or inherited some special gifts.

He'd long been mulling over what she had told him about will power. To set the scene, one evening over a late supper at a small trattoria totally empty except for the two of them, he told her about the mysterious forces in the universe, the dark matter that makes up most of the world's mass, at least 90% of which astronomers have never seen.

"And even those particles millions of light years away have sexual connotations. There are machos and wimps."

Happy smiled.

Only later, when he knew more, did he realize it was a secretive little grin that hints: I know a bit more of mysterious forces in the universe.

"Hey, how come you know so much about astronomy?" she said.

"I just know," he said. "I know a lot. I know more than I think I know," then after a long pause added, "more or less."

"You're an astronomer . . . and you don't want to brag. . . ."

"I'm not."

"How come they're called machos and wimps. . . .?"

"It's complicated—they're actually acronyms—but I'll try. You see, what prevents everything around us from breaking up—like what keeps my bed together, my wardrobe together. . . ."

"Glue?"

"Almost, but not quite. You got the first letter right: gravity. And there are particles we aren't really sure exist which are called wimps, short for Weakly Interacting Massive Particles. You follow?"

"I think."

"Now, as for machos. These are dead stars that still give light, but—forgive the unintentional pun—that's another matter. Astronomers think that machos, short for Massive Compact Halo

Objects, are in galactic halos, capish?"

"Somewhat. Okay. I can see now what holds the wardrobe together. Gravity. Maybe with a little bit of wimpo macho glue. But what holds us together?"

"Me. Maybe with a little bit of you."

"In other words, the wimp and the macho."

Now. Now was the time to ask her:

"And you, do you have any mysterious forces, any secrets, in you?"

Without any prelims, without hesitating, without putting finger to cheek to fake cogitation, she declared straight out:

"I have a magic in me. I think you sense that. Maybe even know it. It's not always there but it comes in surges, like power in high tension lines."

"Give me an example."

"For instance, once a snake bit me and it died."

"And I," Tom parodied her, assuming she was joking, "flowers wilt when I hold them. At my windowsill popinjays shriek and magpies squall. When I look at them, butterflies turn back into moths."

Not a dent on her did make this fantastic litany. So between salad and pasta Tom tried another approach.

"And me, if I bite you, what will happen to me?"

Happy closed her eyes and said as if in a trance:

"An elixir will flow into you and you will fall in love with me forever."

Just then, as if he'd already bitten her, a surge of love and passion he could not see but felt came over him. He sensed a stirring in his loins, his fingers tingling, longing to cling to her breasts, his mouth to be on her thighs, as her magic inundated him in waves of ether.

"Where'd you learn all this?"

"At home. But sometimes I felt so miserable. . . ."

"I got the impression you had a happy childhood."

"So so. There's no such thing as total happiness; when you're sick, you forget health. . . . Sometimes I felt so miserable I wanted to disappear."

"You mean run away?"

"No. Disappear. Vanish. Make myself unseen."

"Not so easy to do."

"Well, if you practice hard it can be done."

He let it pass. It was too absurd to pursue. He let so many of her remarks pass. Like her snake that dropped dead. Her magic elixir. He looked at Happy, eyebrows raised. Replayed her words. There was a primitive stubbornness in her voice as she said all this. Her face was set with the passion of believers in idols, totems, or miraculous images. And, anyway, he was up to dessert. The dessert cart was in front of him, and when faced with three tiers of cakes, tarts, mousses and miniature pies, someone could have told him that the man in the moon was in the back room giving autographs and he wouldn't have budged.

4. On Becoming Invisible

The next day he sits with her on the same vaporetto on which he saw her sailing away that first day, but this time, snared, caught, she's with him, slowly floating up the Grand Canal. All is well with them. He's focusing on Happy; Zoe is only in the back of his mind and not insisting on inching to the front what with Festa approaching and memories of spending that glorious Festa day and night with Zoe, and somehow in the back of his febrile, image-laden mind, his head burdened with petals of Zoe, like a coffin buried under wreaths and scores of flowers, he sits, breathing calmly, thinking to himself: Happy's nice, she's sweet, well, maybe the sweetness has an acerbic edge, but her sexiness makes up for it, she's even gorgeous, you might say, in a limited way, but what was special about her? Wasn't that a question his parents would ask? Wasn't that a question they always asked about many things, books and art and people too? Nothing special, frankly, he knew, she was nothing special. Another run-of-the-mill girl with the erotic gifts of a much older woman. But otherwise nothing special. Zoe, edging to the front of his mind, was something special.

"I owe it all to my mother," Happy suddenly said, as if giving the lie to his negative thoughts. "She taught me a few things when I was young. Like changing the color of my eyes from light blue to brown."

"Special lenses? To make you special."

"No."

"Really?"

"If you don't believe me, you'll see by the end of the evening."

"Like you did with your hair?"

"Uh-huh."

Even from black and white pictures she had shown him one could see she had blue eyes. But the little witch was right. At the end of the evening, under the light of a trattoria, he saw her eyes were brown.

"Okay," he said. "Let's see the brown lenses."

"What brown lenses?"

"Those special colored contact lenses girls use."

"Not me."

"You went to the bathroom and changed lenses."

"Have I left you side all evening?. . . . Look!"

She pulled her lids open with two fingers. The fingers were thick and stubby he saw for the first time. Low-class fingers. "See if you can find a contact lens there."

He looked. Saw nothing. "How did you do it?"

"I once told you. Will power. Concentration."

"Can you make them blue again?"

"Don't you like me with brown eyes?"

"Sure."

"'Sure, but' you wanted to say."

"You always know what I want to say. Sure. But it makes me uncomfortable."

"Why?"

"Because it's weird. It reminds me of the opening of Andre Segovia's *Confessions of Felix Krylov*, where at the beginning the hero practices dilating his iris without the benefit of light. But can you change them back?"

"Yes. But only if you believe I can."

"I do," he lied.

"Okay. I'll change them back. By tomorrow morning they'll be blue again."

"Any other tricks?"

"Yes. I can make myself invisible."

"Wha? Wait a minute! Whoa there!"

But she was quite serious. Not an ironic smile on her face. Not a know-it-all smirk lining any part of her face that would hint: I'm pulling your leg.

"May I hear that absurd assertion once again?"

"Yes. I can make myself invisible."

"Like in a fairy tale?"

"Uh-huh. But unlike a fairy tale this is true. It's no fairy tale."

"Would you do it for me?" he heard himself saying, suddenly seeing Zoe hovering in front of his eyelids. Again Zoe. Another invisible woman. He didn't want to chase her away, back to the back of his mind. After all, the magic triangle. In his big heart, years long and yards wide, there was plenty of room for both. He was an atom that could be in two places at the same time. But the more Happy spoke, the more Zoe invaded and Happy receded, though her voice was still there. The voice was Happy's voice, but her face was starting to look like Zoe's. "Please do it for me," he told her, urging her to stay, not disappear.

"No," Happy said. "It's not for show. Only for when needed."

"You mean you can actually strip yourself of materiality? Like something out of storybooks?"

She tilted her head and spread her hands as if to say: It happens.

"But there is a problem. I can make myself invisible easily enough, but sometimes I forget the fourth word of the formula that brings me back. Then I have to wrack my brains till it comes to me."

"Can't you write it down?" Tom asked. Wait a minute, he told himself. I'm falling into the trap of believing her.

Happy laughed. "I can't carry it with me."

"Can someone whisper it to you, like a prompter?"

"No. I can't hear when I'm invisible. . . . Like right now, I'm trying to think of it and I can't even remember the first syllable." She shrugged and smiled as if that were one of the occupational hazards.

"Any other feats?" he asked. But seeing her hesitation, he added, "I mean tricks."

"Sometimes I do astral projections but I'm not very good at that. . . ." he heard her say from a distance.

"What does it involve?" he said, sensing that the more he asked about magic the more she changed and the clearer Zoe's image became, as though his words were the developing solution bringing a faint image into sharp focus. Now that both were before him he saw similarities between them he hadn't noticed before. Or was his vision clouded by the magic she was describing? He wanted to keep asking questions, for his words were an elixir, his speech a magic spell. Some words he didn't even hear, but the magic of words about magic had a magical effect.

"It involves concentration, yoga-like breathing exercises, mirror gazing. . . ."

Mirror gazing, he thought. That's my specialty.

"Do you do that?" he asked.

"I don't have the energy or the concentration for that."

"Did your mother teach you this too?" He barely heard his

words. They came out a whisper, a gasp. And then he felt his breath leaving him, as though after a failed test on how long he could hold his breath. But he wasn't testing himself. Someone else was holding his breath. He felt he was going to faint. His breaths grew shallower, shorter, as if Happy's words were compressing his windpipe, squeezing his lungs, hardly able to breathe, and the more she spoke the fainter he felt, but the more she looked like Zoe—was becoming Zoe, finally was Zoe standing before him down to the little birthmark on the side of her cheek—the less he breathed. So his wish to see Zoe was coming true but at the expense of his breath, his life, his being, having all of Zoe just when there was nothing left of him.

"I got it from my mother without her teaching me. I got it from her skin. Her warmth. Her hugs."

Keep the questions coming he told himself. Keep the interview alive, said an inner voice. Ask, ask. Make believe it's billiards or aerobics. Bounce the ball, bounce yourself.

But now it wasn't he who was asking. It was the demon within him seeking to have her talk about magic.

"How does this jibe with wanting to disappear?"

"Life isn't all misery, you know. It's a mix. Good moments and bad. I remember both."

So do I, Zoe, he thought. "How was your trip?" he asked Zoe.

Happy laughed. "That wasn't misery at all. It was great."

Suddenly she took three sharp little breaths, leaned her head back and sneezed three times demurely—"ptsee, ptsee, ptsee"—holding her mouth, then pulled her right earlobe three times.

"She also taught me that. . . . I told you the other day it's for good luck. She said if you sneezed and you happen to be talking or thinking about something bad, like illness or death, it would come true. Because it's the body and soul's way of saying, Yes, that's what's going to happen. But by tugging your earlobe, it undoes it, don't ask me why, it just does. It also helps to counteract if someone is thinking bad of you when you are sneezing. . . . Sneezing is a very mysterious thing."

That's what you were thinking of me, bad, Zoe told him. But it was your fault.

"Do you really believe that?" Tom asked her.

"Not personally. . . . But it can't hurt," Happy said.

"Were you thinking of something bad?" Tom asked her.

She didn't want to say.

"Say it. I'm not superstitious. Were you?"

"I don't want to say it," Happy said.

"Say it!"

She took a deep breath and he felt again his breath was being sucked away, losing consciousness—Happy breathing his air.

"I thought something awful is going to happen and you'll leave me."

Now he was hearing duets. Zoe and Happy reciting the words together. Why was Happy ventriloquizing through Zoe's mouth? Happy seemed to be there but was not. Or rather, Zoe seemed not to be there but was.

He reached across the distance of space and tugged three times on her earlobe.

"I thought you weren't superstitious," she said.

"I'm not. But it can't hurt, Specially if it's your ears I'm tugging. . . ." Keep the questions coming, Zoe told him. Ask. Ask. "What else did your mom teach you?"

"That tarot cards contain secrets of the universe. You should meet her. You'd love her. She knows spells and runes. She's mastered mysterious forces."

That's why you're before me now, Zoe, because of Happy's mother's powers. But wasn't Zoe being called before him through nether powers, like Margarita for Faust through Mephisto? He wasn't much of a believer, but he knew that using black arts meant danger and, worse, evanescence. But when a person is desperate, a straw is a plank, a sugar cube a cure-all. The more Happy spoke of her mother's magical arts, the better he felt, like harps and organs playing. A beautiful musical nexus was being created between them. An engine being fed and creating for him Zoe. Just words, but these had a potency that vivified his longing, his incendient imagination.

If she's mastered these forces, he didn't ask, how come your dad still has to run a small Albany restaurant and your mom is in a hole-in-the-wall fortuneteller's booth?

"But she didn't do it for personal gain," Happy said. "She loves her work. There's lots more mysterious things in this world than we know about. For instance, did you know about the poet-magicians in Albania who rhyme or versify their victims to death? Do you know how? You don't. They chant satiric poems about them till black, red and white blotches and blisters erupt on their skin which makes them die."

"What's your secret?" he asked her, at least he thought he asked her, although it was possible, even likely, that instead of saying it, he heard it, someone asking him if he had a secret. And if he heard it, who said it? Zoe or Happy? He had to know, because there would be a different answer for each person, even though the question was the same. Wasn't it like that V he loved so much? It stemmed from one same point, but went out into two different directions. So his secret. It was imbedded at the point of the V, but that one point radiated out to two different spheres: Zoe or Happy. Why did he have to be a V? Why couldn't he be an I? Why was everything on two levels with him? The apparent and the real, the visible and the phantasmagoric, text and subtext. He knew that logically Happy should be before him. He was glad to be with her but would not blink away Zoe who the more he spoke the more she materialized before him. And the more Happy spoke about magic the more subtext overrode text, fantasy the visible, the apparent the real. As Zoe, not Happy, stood now before him.

"I'm so glad you came to Venice," he told Zoe. "I've been waiting ages for you."

"Now isn't that romantic!" said Happy.

Why did she have to direct attention to herself now? Why did Happy have to talk and kill the mood? Now he was back on earth again.

"And in your mom's studio, she has the crystal ball and the tea leaves, a lit candle, the entire getup?"

"*Three* lit candles. Perfumed to make the air smell good."

Three, he thought. One for me, one for you, and one for her. The magic triangle, the potent threesome, the classic family. Us. Now. Looking for each other.

"And the crystal ball?"

"Of course the crystal ball, which is absolutely worthless, but she can't do without it, the customers expect it. The entire getup you say? My mom also had a shrinking charm but it got lost. She would write *Abracadabra* on one line and on the next line one letter less and so on till you got the line which only had an *A* and then you could read the word every which way and then you wear it in a little cloth bag around your neck for three times three days and nights and then throw it over your left shoulder without look-ing."

"And this shrinks pimples, hemorrhoids."

"Who said anything about hemorrhoids?"

"Then what does it shrink?"

"Your enemy's anger away."

At that, once more, he felt himself gasping for breath. Happy had thrown the reverse triangle *Abracadabra* over her shoulder and it hit him and his breath was shrinking. But then she must have tugged at her earlobe or pressed her nose, for just as quickly his breath returned, the faintness gone.

"Did you ever visit her in her what-do-you-call-it, shop, stu-dio, booth, atelier?"

"She never let me come there."

"Then I have a question. How shall I put it to you? You know witchcraft has always been associated with lascivious sexual prac-tices. Do you think she ran a...you know?"

"No, no, no, no! Stop it!" Happy's face contorted. "I with-draw the invitation for you to meet my mother. You're insulting her. Us. Me."

"Sorry." He tried to soften his tone, but he had to keep asking for Zoe was fading. "Did she do dolls and pins?"

"No. She read tea leaves, wax meltings, but she didn't do buri-als of wax shapes to give a customer power over his victim. She didn't do trances, voodoo, or speak in tongues. For that you have to specialize?"

"A kind of voodoo internship," he laughed. Now he felt good again. Still seeing Zoe. Where did he go during those moments that he blanked out? Did she notice it? And who was this "she"? Was it Zoe or Happy, or both in one? Now he saw how much one resembled the other. Why hadn't he noticed it before? You might even say that they looked alike. He couldn't point to an affinity, of let's say vertical lines down each cheek like Happy maintained that both she and he had in common, or the slightly arched brows, or the full kiss-me, kiss-me lips. Still, he noticed the resemblance even with his breath stuck in his throat, he still more in the next world than in this one. Anyone with vision could see it's Zoe! Zoe! Zoe!

Stay, fair spirit, permit me to approach. Out of my way, demons and sprites, for I'll make a ghost of him that lets me!

Happy laughed too. "Sort of. But she didn't do anything to hurt. She never predicted bad but believed if you predicted good a person's will would work in that direction."

"A kind of natural psychologist."

"I suppose. . . . Any other questions? I feel like I'm being interviewed for *Astrology Today.* . . . ." Then she began muttering.

"What?"

"Can you imagine, all of a sudden it's on the tip of my tongue. . . . I feel it rolling around in there."

"What is?"

"The fourth word of the formula. Cam . . . can . . . canner . . . kidoo. . . . No, it's not there."

Happy looked thoughtful; blinked; had a faraway look.

Tom rocked on his heels, holding back his next question. *Don't go, Zoe!*

Then Happy suddenly said loudly, "Kincannerdoo. . . . That's it! That's the last word. I got it." She smiled happily. "Now I'm ready to be invisible. Want to see? I'm ready to try it out for you."

She was reversing the tables on him. First he wanted to see her become invisible and she refused, and now she was offering it to him. If he said yes, she might whine:

And what if I don't remember the last word this time? I'll be stuck. Invisible forever. You'd like that.

No. I would not. Why in the world do you say that?

Then why do you want me to take this chance?

It was your suggestion, remember?

"No, thanks," Tom said. "Suppose you really do forget it. And then what am I going to do when I want to hold you? Squeeze air?"

"I won't forget. Wanna see? I haven't done it for a long time, ever since I got away from a rapist. . . . So? . . . Shall I?"

"No," he said. "Save it for when it counts."

"You sure?"

"Sure I'm sure." Zoe nudged him. *Ask her another question. Quick!* "But there's one more thing. I once read about burying a doll image. What happens when you do that?" He looked up. Zoe still hovered there.

"By doing that you hope your enemy will suffer the same agony. By imitating an event you hope to make it happen. Or at least it makes you feel good. But that's bad. My mother told me never to end with something bad when I talk about her. So I'll tell you something nice. She told me that every person has a song in his heart and the purpose of life is to release that song before he dies. Trouble is people never live long enough for that song to be released. . . . Wait a minute!. . . . That's bad again." She put her arms around him. "Hold me. Kiss me. . . . That's good."

He held her and kissed her and it was good. But he didn't call Zoe by her name.

When Happy left him to go back to her pensione, he lay on his bed, staring up at the dark ceiling. As soon as she left Zoe went away too. And now it was dark. In the room and in his soul. But the ceiling wasn't completely dark, not as dark as his soul anyway, because in Venice no matter how dark it was there was always light. There was so much light in Venice it seeped into the darkest corners and made them glow. He replayed his encounter with Happy in his mind. Happy invisible. He shook his head. What next? Me and Tarzan will play Mozart's Concerto for Two Pianos at the La Fenice Theatre.

He tried to reason out her invisibility. This wasn't the Middle Ages where alchemists reigned, and he wasn't in a special effects film! There had to be a rational explanation. Then it came to him, in the glowing darkness. Secrets. Secrets, he concluded, dragged man down, gave bones and sinews, pins and cloth to the see-through spirit, the no-frills soul. He had a secret and that was why he was visible. That was why everybody was visible—because they had secrets. But Happy had no secrets. She was open; her soul was crystalline. That's why, he reasoned, she could be invisible. The more secrets one had, the more earthbound one became.

Secrets were our gravity.

5. The Mirror

Yes. Tom had a secret. There were secrets and secrets. There were secrets that snoozed between the eyes, above the bridge of the nose, and there were secrets enmeshed in the fibers of the heart. He knew which kind was his. That secret never left him, but he never spoke of it, especially to himself. This was the first time he even admitted to himself that he had a secret. And that was why he was in Venice. Was he willing to say it out loud? To tell it to himself while making faces in the mirror. To tell it to Happy, to free himself of gravity and become crystalline like her? No way!, one voice within him shouted. Maybe!, shouted another. Maybe her magic can pave the way.

Magic, at least in her telling, clung to her. All during her life, said she, strange phenomena (not her word) appeared in her presence. For instance, the left-handed cup.

"What left-handed cup?"

"Listen and you'll find out."

Happy took a deep breath and paused for a moment, hoping for dramatic effect.

"I once was working as a salesgirl in an Albany gift shop and a guy comes in and asks for a left-handed cup. I mean, he says, I want to buy a nice cup and saucer for a friend of mine who's a lefty. So I show him a cup and a saucer and he points to the handle on the right and says, 'That's for a righty.' I couldn't believe my ears. I try not to roll my eyes in exasperation at this jerk. So I turn the cup around and say, 'Now it's for a lefty.' 'Wait a minute,' the guy says, 'don't try to put one over on me. I'm not buying a cup made for a righty'; and he switches it back to the right-hand position. Meantime, the boss has come by and is hearing this. Now he's a guy with an intellectual bent, self-educated, you know, you remind me of him, and he tells the guy, I'll demonstrate with an allergy. He picks up a little rectangular mirror and shows it to the guy. 'You see your face here?' The jerk says yes. 'Okay, now if I turn the mirror upside down, are you upside down?' The jerk doesn't even look but says—he's not so stupid after all, just a bit loony, or maybe just stupid along certain lines—so he says, 'What's that got to do with a left-handed cup?' So my boss answers, 'To show you by an allergy that by reversing position it makes no difference whatsoever. So look, look, now that I'm holding the mirror the other way, do you see yourself upside down?' Now the jerk looks and says, you won't believe this, I almost fainted when I heard him say, 'Yes!' 'What?' my boss yells and his voice is shaking and he tells me to go around the corner of the counter and see if the guy is telling the truth. My boss is still holding the mirror and his hand, like his voice, is trembling a bit. I go around to the other side of the counter and guess what I see? The guy's face *is* upside down. 'Okay,' the guy says smugly. 'Now can you recommend a store that sells left-handed cups?' and before we have a chance to recover he says, 'But I'll take the mirror. How much?'

"But the manager wouldn't sell it. He clutched it to his heart like it was a living thing. Later, when I stopped working for him, he gave it to me. Just like that. Wouldn't take a penny. Wanna see it?"

It was a trick, he knew. A trick mirror. He knew it by the sound of her voice, by that chin-up challenge. "Wanna see it?" She went for her pocketbook, pulled out a little something in a black velvet bag and held it up like a trophy. "It's in here."

"And what if I do?" he said, thinking: This'll bring her down a notch, showing me that the trick mirror and nothing happening.

"But it will only work once. You look at it once, you'll see yourself upside down. Next time you use it, it will reflect like a normal mirror."

"Never mind," he said.

"I keep it in this little black bag in my pocketbook. Anytime you want to look, it's yours."

6. *Happy Flirtatious, Happy on Fire*

Good things, too-good-to-be-true things, have a short half life. One day at a trattoria they had been to before he saw her looking ga-ga eyed straight into the eyes of a waiter as she discussed— what do you mean *discussed*; it was no discussion; it was provocative laughter; open flirtation—the menu choices with him. He had never seen that look on her face before. A blister opened up in his heart, as if somewhere in the mountains of Albania (read: the side streets of Albany) some bard were versifying lines directed at him, and out came the pus of jealousy. And as that venom coursed through him, the more couplets the Albanian rhymester execrated at him the more he began to understand. She and the waiter were playing that game before his eyes, savoring their secret which was a secret no longer. Now she can't even hide her longing for the guy. She's gotten to know him, the bitch. She's carrying on with him right in front of me behind my back. Furious, he bit his lip and tried to keep a moderate tone as he spoke to her:

He didn't like what she did, he told her. He wasn't the sort to hold back, to dam up the feeling and tell someone else: You know what she did? We're at this trattoria which, my God, I took her to a number of times and she has the gall to look the waiter in the eye as she's ordering; staring straight into his eyes, locking eyes with him, seeing no one else, certainly not me, it was an intimate look as if they've known each other for years. Maybe she had. But he won't frustrate himself, he said, by telling a third party about this. He was telling it to her straight out, and yes, you could call it a tone of reproach. How could you do this to me? Giving him that loving look.

It wasn't loving, she said. You're making a molehill out of an anthill, or something like that.

Okay, so it wasn't loving, so it was adoring. Locking eyes with him. You could have gone into a dance with him, oblivious to everyone else around you.

But she defended herself. She didn't intend to flirt, she . . .

What's the difference if you intended to or not? Fact is you did. If I could have put a thermometer on that glance it would have zoomed up to 180°.

Oh, it would not have, she said with a straight face. Maybe 150° maximum.

Get a new thermometer. If I had filmed this, my Lord, all we needed was background music and we could have had a scene from *Casablanca*. Ingrid Bergman and Bogey.

You are making a scene, she said.

As long as it's not from *Casablanca*, he said.

It's not worth fighting, she said.

Okay, he said, but he couldn't stop the camera. Maybe she knew him from somewhere, runs through his mind. Maybe they had a fling before she met him. And maybe she's having one right now. It was a knowing look. God, if she'd seen herself looking at him like that she'd have blushed with shame.

You should have seen yourself in the mirror giving him that look. You'd have been embarrassed. But then again, anyone who could flash a smile like that has no shame to begin with. I'll tell you what, and that 'I'll tell you what', delivered in a different tone, caught her off guard, just as he hoped it would. Tell you what, sounding as if it were a neat compromise offered by a neutral third party, which made her perk up, for though he didn't see them closed, he knew she had closed her ears like a moose closing his nose flaps under water. Tell you what, you can look at him as much as you want—now wasn't that a nice compromise offer, a gentlemanly approach? Wide, wide, now wide open were her ears— but if I see him looking at you like that again, I'm going to throw him to the canal, do you understand?

He looked at her and wondered what her reaction would be. She could have told him to mind his own business; she could have told him, Tell it to him, not me; she could have told him she can't control other people's looks; she could have told him, Bug off! But maybe, he thought, she took his outburst as an expression of love, of protectiveness. Girls have been known to react that way.

She said meekly, Yes.

But even that, alas, didn't satisfy him. Jealousy sews tight your eyes, clamps shut your ears, glues your tongue to the roof of your mouth and pinches your nostrils till you're blue in the face. He didn't like her Yes. He wasn't sure she meant it, for it was a mat-ter-of-fact, moderately pitched Yes. It wasn't a whispered, roman-tic, open-eyed, soft, suppliant, submissive, I'll-do-anything-for-you-darling "Yes," said with a starry-eyed innocence that promised absolute fidelity with Mischa Elman playing Beethoven's *Romanza for Violin* softly in the background. No. He thought he heard a forked tongue saying Yes. He heard a duplicity in that Yes, maybe because two ears—a doubled, duplicitous hearing—heard that Yes.

We're fighting, and it's the first time, she said, with a sharp sizzle in her voice, her words like thin pinpricks, missiles blown through a straw.

We're not.

We are and I don't like it.

She doesn't like it, he says to himself. What about what I don't like? Maybe she's slutty. Completely undependable. No loyalty. Will flirt with another guy in your presence. Like in his dream, will screw your friend and say it was great. What can one expect from such low class stock? And her mama was probably a madam on the side.

Maybe it's not a fight, he told her, but an expression of the elemental forces in the world in conflict, the pull between Ying and yang, ping and pong, yip and yap, see and saw. If Ying is up, yang is down, Jung is out. One can't ping and pong at the same time. See and saw are in tension as they are in grammar. Only in a Euclidean universe where parallel bars bend down for midgets do both ends of the see-saw point up. You're too smart for me, she said. I don't mean smart-smart, that I am too, in a more limited way, I guess, but I can compete. I mean smart-*smart*. You know things, you look at things with a different set of eyes and it makes me feel creepy, like your Chinese philosophy of ping and pong and your Klitty Anne universe, I don't know what you're talking about.

But if he was suspicious of her, what kept him interested? Simple. Not her mind, which was neither cultured nor cultivated, but agile and street-smart. Her head sent her tongue more messages than her mind. It was her glorious body, slim waist, flat tummy, enormous boobs, her sexual panache, her quirky personality. She didn't have to go to school for screwing. In that she was a classic autodidact, a fucking first-class act. In fact, she could open up a correspondence school of her own. He had never felt such a kinship, a closeness, the heat of desire during connubia as with

Happy. Not even with Zoe. With Happy he felt an extension of himself and given the myth, as they looked into the mirror and pressed faces together (he acting out one half of the old theater joke of the veteran acting couple who were absolutely and totally in love, she with herself, he with himself), that they had some similar facial lineaments, each supporting the other's remark, "We look like each other," gaining support for this by constant repetition till they got to believe it (like many remarks that are not true but are perceived as true by replication).

He couldn't put his finger on it. His hands, yes; his finger, no. Entwined with her, he felt weightless with love, felt himself whirling in some extra-terrestrial spin. She never said no. Never felt ill or faint or didn't feel like it. The minute they were alone in his room they were all over each other. He lay back on the bed. In a trice, she was on top of him. Until they changed positions, on their sides, she in front, he behind. "Oh, it's you," she jokes over her shoulder, turning her head to him, "Hi, there!" "Didn't you know it was me? I mean, who were you expecting?" catching himself before he said, "The waiter?" "Well, I wasn't facing traffic," she said. The kid was constantly on fire. So much so that that too, *magari*, as they say in Italian, caused him problems. As usual, too good is no good; or as the Venetians say, the bride is too beautiful. He wondered, alas, if she was this way with every guy and if that look she gave the waiter that day was a look she gave everyone and that her desire was totally hers and not inspired by him. But when he was with her, the intensity of her eroticism, her animal pleasure, ignited him too to climb rungs on a ladder, rungs that weren't there. It was as if their contiguous globes of pleasure, his and hers, slowly interlocked, and like molecules joining, became one.

Was it possible that he was angry at Happy because he was angry at Zoe, suspicious of her and her motives and declarations even after so many years, mixing them up in his mind because his mind mixed them up for him, having one intrude when he was thinking of the other, as if there was an inexorable link between them? Oh, if he could only rewrite the past he'd be the greatest historian in the world—setting wrongs aright and reversing bad decisions, even making time stand still. With him as author, there would be no need to taste life twice. Once would be enough.

7. How Sweet the Feeling When the Fight Is Forgotten

When he said goodbye to her, he held her in his arms and said: "Like Shakespeare said, Good night, sweet princess, parting is such sad honey."

And once she was out the door, he, wearing suspicion like a comfortable old sweater, he followed her home. Maybe she's meeting the waiter. Maybe her affection for me is all bluff. A cover. As he gets to the foot of a little bridge and she has to turn either left or right, he thinks she does both and instead of following one of the two Happys, he's paralyzed and rooted.

The next day, in bed, she said—and her lips hardly moved; it was as if she'd become a ventriloquist—hissing:

"Why'd you follow me yesterday?"

Which caused him to gag in more ways than one.

"How'd you know?"

"I have a rear view mirror on my glasses."

"But you don't wear glasses."

"That's exactly what I mean."

At first he thought of denying it, but he right away confessed: "I'm so crazy about you, I couldn't take the idea of you seeing anyone else. . . . How did you become two people? I didn't know which Happy to follow."

"Trick mirrors," she said. "Rear view mirror. Upside down mirror. It's smoke and mirrors that run your Klitty Anne universe."

They fought and they made up. So sweet was the calm after the storm; it drew them even closer. They were so intertwined with each other when they slept together on her two mornings off a week, his leg between hers, her leg around his, her left arm around his waist, his right around hers, it took them half the following morning to sort out their limbs, for each to reclaim his own. Once he noticed he walked with a limp, wondered why. They had inadvertently changed legs and he had her leg on for several hours before he noticed.

Happy goes off in two directions and Tommy doesn't even have one.

In the dark before dawn when the soul is awake and the body fast asleep and the soul directs questions at the body, he wondered which direction his life would take. The Festa was approaching. The terminus date. The grand celebration—before what? Ecstasy or let-down? He remembered a line from Chaucer's *Troilus*: All steerless within a boat am I amid the sea, tossed to and fro betwixt two winds. One Zoe, one Happy.

Next morning, Happy, highly charged with ESP, surprised him with another question. He wondered what was happening with her. Has her brain gotten a new spurt of cogitational cells?

She asked: "Are you searching for anything?"

"You mean here?" he said, startled.

"Here. There. Anywhere."

"You read my mind, you witch. . . . Don't tell me you know Chaucer?"

She smiled seductively. "Is that the waiter's name?"

He let it pass. "I was just thinking of that, that search. If I were asked to sum it up in a word, I could."

He stopped.

Happy looked at him. "Well?"

"I wasn't asked to sum it up in a word."

"I'm asking. Can you sum it up in a word?"

"Yes."

"What is it?"

"Ecstasy. And I found it with you."

Tom listened to the sound of his words in the echo chamber of his memory. Their music was flat. Passionless. Maybe not without passion, but certainly not with. In other words, Tommy Manning, you're not telling the truth. The truth, he replied, is not always in words. Words can say one thing, the heart another. What I'm telling her is halfway between truth and deception. But the show must go on, right? So he continued the playacting that was somewhere between rehearsal and show.

"A kind of transcendent quality that fuses the personal and the sexual. It's a floating without leaving the ground. A high without narcotics, alcohol or plants. . . . Do you know what 'transcendent' is?"

"Yes. It's like 'descendant', only the other way."

"Very funny."

"Why do you have to talk down to me?" She suddenly turned on him. Perhaps she caught the hesitation in his voice, sensed his rumination. Saw him adrift twixt to and fro; saw his gondola rudderless between two winds. "Does it give you a special pleasure?"

He felt his face flushing.

"Me? I don't talk down to you."

"You don't, huh? Like the other day at the Bach concert and me not being able to spell. You must think I'm some kind of special idiot."

"You're not special at all. . . . No, that doesn't ring too well, does it?. . . What I meant to say was: You're not a *special* idiot. . . . I mean there's nothing special about your idiocy. I mean it won't win any prizes in a national contest. . . . Oh, never mind. . . . Give me an example of how I talk down to you. . . . I can't hear you.... Wanna come up a bit on the ladder. . . . Careful, watch your step. . . . The fact that I ask you about a word that you surely don't know and neither does 90% of the population, rather than have you pitch it over your shoulder at me as you're leaving like you usually do, should be taken as an exemplar of my consideration for you and not as emblematic of my conceit."

"There you go again, purposely, with your fancy words that drives me up the wall. And you do this snob-speak so naturally you even do it when we're making love."

"What are you talking about? When was that?"

"When? I'll tell you when. . . . Like you tell me, 'I'm going to kiss every part of your body. Just tell me where to begin and if you can't pronounce it, just point.'"

"But you laughed," he said.

"Sure, I laughed. But it hurt me. . . . And you laughed too."

"Sure, I laughed. But it hurt."

"It hurt me more."

"So why didn't you cry?" he asked her.

"Because I'd rather laugh."

"So don't complain. . . . I only meant it to be funny."

"At my expense."

He took out his tiny calculator and pretended to punch in a few numbers. As soon as he turned it on, it reminded him of the date of Festa night.

"What're you doing?"

"Figuring out the expenses," he said, wondering what Happy would do on Festa that night when, as he told her at the beginning, he had his long-standing appointment. Me and my big mouth, suddenly went through his head. Right away I had to go and show off about my knowledge of Venetian life and tell her about the Festa. But she would have found out about it anyway. How could one live in Venice and not know about it? It's like being oblivious to Christmas while living in New York in December. But that's probably a big night for the folks at the pensione and he was sure that Happy would have to baby-sit for her bosses' kid that Sunday night, so there was no need to worry.

She stood before him, hands on her hips.

"You know, you don't like me," she declared and suddenly began bawling. Little crystal tears dropped from her eyes, one by one.

He opened his mouth to protest, to inveigh against the injustice of her remark, but nothing came out. He made a couple of fish-like snaps with his mouth, then managed to say:

"Like you! I don't like you—I . . . but no, you're not going to use that method to fish for compliments."

"You may love me but you don't like me."

"My philosophical, nay, my morphological sense, doesn't permit me to digest this oxymoron."

"Which means what in everyday English?... My God, we can't even communicate with you any more. Lately you've started talking middy evil English."

"Methinks you mean Middle English, forsooth. . . . What I said before simply means that you're absurd."

"But you haven't said you like me. Okay, you don't deny it. At least we got that much established. . . . So if you had to make a list of things you don't like about me, how would you begin?"

"One. I don't like you telling me to make a list of things I don't like about you."

"Fine. . . . Two?"

"Two? I didn't think there's more than one."

"Force yourself."

He thought about it, of what happened the other day. She should know a little more about music. But she told him she knew next to nothing about music, even as he was buying tickets to the Bach Brandenburg concert. She even seemed proud of it, wore her ignorance like a medallion on her attractive chest. Only rarely had she gone to a concert before she met him, she said. Well, to be perfectly frank, only once. And even then, by mistake, thinking it was a pop singer. In Albany, she had seen an ad for an all-Franck program and thought it would be Sinatra. In fact, she wondered why the prices were so low. "And why they misspelled his name," he interjected. "But that you probably didn't notice." Once, during the intermission, when everyone went out to the Campo for a walk, he decided he'd play a little game with her, act out a comic dialogue in a great novel he'd read some years back. As usual, he couldn't remember the author's name and was vague about the title, something like *Passion in the Desert*, or maybe *A Passion for Desserts*, but the words he remembered almost photographically. In one scene the hero who adores music takes a girl who knows nothing to her first classical concert and pulls her leg about various composers.

"You heard of the three B's?" he asked Happy.

"Sure."

"Let's hear them."

"Bumble bee, spelling bee and... um... quilting bee."

"Very good, but not quite. I mean B as first initial of famous...."

"Oh yeah, okay. I get it. The Bulls, the Braves and the Buffalo Bills."

"Very funny. Try Bach, Beethoven and Brahms."

"Who do they play for?" Happy asked.

"Even funnier. . . . Anyway, the first performance of this Bach Brandenburg concerto we just heard had the three B's in the orchestra and it was guest conducted by Bartok."

"How come Bach didn't conduct? He wrote it."

"Very good. You're learning already and intermission isn't even over yet. It's because Bach by then was an old man and blind. He had twenty-two children but blindness was no impediment. Poor man went blind from too much solo polo, if you know what I mean."

She said yes, she knew what he meant. But the fact that she didn't smile showed him that she didn't know what he meant at all.

"You know so much about music," Happy said.

He was delighted with her compliment but said modestly, "Not enough."

"But you have bees in your bonnet."

How he would have wanted to be an expert on old-time opera singers, for instance, and, like some people he knew, identify voices and say: That's Galli-Curci, that's Richard Tucker, that's Beniamino Gigli; cite the aria, the opera, and analyze the singer's gifts and range, where he made his debut and relate some juicy stories about him. He would have wanted to be able to say, when listening to a recording of a violinist, That's Elman's tone, that's Oistrakh, that's Heifetz, that's Perlman.

"Well," Happy insisted, "don't you have anything more for your What I Don't Like About Happy List?"

"Okay. You should get to know a little more about music."

"I'll try. Is that all?"

"Yes. Squeeze, choke me, slay me, I can't come up with another flaw. Otherwise, you're nearly perfect."

"Nearly? Then who's perfect?"

He smiled benignly at her. "Modesty doesn't permit me to say."

Then he took her by the hand, cocked his head toward the bed.

"No," she said. "I can only respect a man with flaws. And since you're perfect, I can't respect you. And I can't sleep with a man I don't respect."

"I never dreamt that there could be spontaneous generation of an Aristotelian syllogism, but you've done it."

"You're talking middy evil English again."

"So you can't sleep with a man you can't respect, huh?"

"Right."

"And I'm just the opposite. I can't respect a girl I can't sleep with."

"Then we both agree," she said in a huff.

He didn't want her to have the last word, but instead of making a statement he stupidly asked a question.

"Why am I always the one who's interested in, and initiates, sex?"

"Because you have a better partner," quoth the little bitch.

8. Face to Face With the Secret

There was a stillness in the air as he walked the deserted Piazza San Marco just before the sun rose. She'll be back, he thought. She loves sex too much. She's the only girl I know who can have an orgasm after sex, just lying next to me and thinking about what she's just had. The air was fresh and clear, as if a mountain breeze had wafted down. Two lone sweepers with old-fashioned straw brooms shaped like a sickle were sweeping the great square. The more they swept the brighter it became—until they swept away the shadows and the empty square was bathed in light.

There was a stillness in his heart, broken by the pounding of blood that unsettled him. Isn't it time for a secret? The secret that Happy had intuited? The secret that his heart kept from his will.

The secret of why Thomas Manning was really in Venice for the Festa, wasn't it time?

Zoe.

Zoe.

Zoe. And no one else.

Zoe was why he was in Venice.

Not business. Not vacation. Not nostalgia. Not reliving again his, or his father's, love for the city.

No one else but Zoe.

Not memory of her, not faint trembling of her, not echoes of her.

But Zoe.

Zoe herself.

No one else but Zoe.

He was looking out the window of his room when the phone rang.

"Tommy."

She didn't raise her voice at the last syllable. She said his name as a declarative, as if pointing him out in a lineup. Despite her soft, baby voice, that "Tommy" pinned him to the wall. Now all he could do was wriggle. Thinking it over, he didn't know why he didn't ask politely, How are you?

"Yes?"

There was no business-lunch polite chit-chat, no verbal foreplay. She went right to the heart of the matter.

She said:

"I'm pregnant."

I'm dreaming, was his first thought, over which another thought was montaged—but which thought really came first is hard to say. His thinking, I'm not here, you're not there, wasn't quite second, but wasn't first either. And over all the thoughts, and over all the jagged currents of words, spurts of fear, thoughts and questions which had no time sequence but hung in space and were conceived all at the same time, lay a darker wish: hang up. And another thought—which wove through the warp of the others, wrinkling them, drawing them into a knot, tangling them so they would not be understood—was: She's lying. Which was immediately wiped out by: Impossible. She'd never do that.

Of course she was joking! Pregnant, my foot! He was about to ring her back to confirm that yes it was all a joke but decided it would be puerile. Of course she was joking. Or lying. She wanted to marry him. She's fallen head over heels, poor kid. Maybe it wasn't even him; it was the romance of Venice, the accretion of layers of romance that happened to fall upon him. For goodness sake, he was only—

"Tommy." That soft, insistent declarative.

Then she called to tell him something else. She wasn't pregnant. She was just kidding. Wanted to see his reaction.

Wanted to see if I was gonna marry you, right?

Right.

I guess I failed the test, but . . .

But don't worry about it, she said. Main thing is I'm not pregnant. I was worried a couple of days, because it was late, and then it came, Whew!!

That's the main thing, he said. Can you imagine the load off my chest?

Yours? How about mine? she said. But I'm only fooling. Had you scared, huh?

Yes, but . . .

But what?

But it was a nasty trick to scare me like that. To put me to the test like in a sting operation, he said.

Would you rather I was *really* pregnant?

No, he said.

Tell me, she continued, what would you have done if I really was pregnant?

We would have gotten together and reasoned it out to both our satisfaction.

"I'm . . ."

But he knew his words were sounds sent by a forked tongue. Did she expect him to drop everything and go out to Cincinnati or Cleveland or wherever she was from and marry her? Start a family, take a job, maybe as assistant manager in a pizza shop, for crying out loud? He could just see himself, he was only twenty-two for goodness sakes, just out of college, about to go to grad school in London, entombed in a pizza parlor when he had the whole wide world open to him. No, there had to be a better way. Maybe it was a mistake. A misdiagnosis. Things like that always happen. Or maybe she was only a little bit pregnant and lots of malteds and jumping exercises would make it vanish, disappear, go away. And anyway, who knows what kind of tricks girls were capable nowadays? So let's think it through, he told himself. What if she is pregnant, like she claims? He had already told her that given both their circumstances there was only one solution; the most practical one; perhaps the least romantic but surely the most practical. But no, she'd been adamant; refused. She said she'd go away, spare her parents embarrassment. But under no circumstances would she kill her baby, their baby. Not so much because she was against abortion on ideological grounds, though she didn't quite use those words, just afraid personally. Actually terrified at the thought of it. She would exercise. Jump up and down, diet and drink, eat a lot or a little, whatever the guidebooks said would induce a natural abortion or a miscarriage or whatever it was called. She recalled reading such things but that if that didn't succeed she would rather have the baby. For deep down, he realized, deep down she *wanted* to have the baby, for all her efforts weren't really sincere. She just went through the motions. Pretending to him, to herself, to the world. Whatever she did, whatever she said, she didn't *mean* it. Not even the jumping up and down. They were just feathery little half-assed ballerina jumps that couldn't dislodge a flake of dandruff, not heavy duty, I-really-mean-it jumps. But still, still, still, he couldn't shake the thought: Maybe she was faking. Maybe it was a false pregnancy. Maybe it would go away. Or *she* would go away. She'd wake up one day and see it's all a dream. Or he'd wake up, rub his eyes, wipe it all away, swift as the flick of a whip, and wish: Make it vanish. Go away.

". . . pregnant."

You see, he tried to explain to her, grad school was waiting, a once-in-a-lifetime opportunity. The pizza shop could wait. It wasn't for him. She understood, she said in her soft baby voice. She'd handle it, she'd go into the dark alone. She knew where they stood, that it was no go for them as a couple. She was on a different level, right? Go ahead, contradict me, she said. He didn't. It was like out of a novel she'd once read. Poor girl, privileged boy. Things could only click briefly and then like a dream disappear. His father was a big landowner; hers a postal clerk. He was going to London to graduate school, would intern for a Member of Parliament, went her narrative, and she dropped out of a county college after two years to go to work and had her once-in-a-lifetime vacation in Europe and had the poor/good luck to meet up with him, and have a week of passion and bliss together, and this is where it leads to. Why was everyone else in the world happy?, she allowed herself this momentary complaint, so unusual for her. This is the path, don't you think I knew that I'd be put on this road, that you'd put me on this road, the minute I dropped my knapsack at Amexco and you, you hesitated for a while, I was watching you, I had my eye on you, you good-looking dude, even though all my things were scattered on the floor, everyone was staring at me as if I was some intruder who'd broken some magic spell, the big bad witch who suddenly appears uninvited, then you came scurrying along as if you wanted to put Humpty Dumpty together again, I knew that it was a path that I'd be sorry I started out on, a path I shouldn't have trodden, Oh why, dammit, why did that knapsack slip out of my hands? And she began, for the first time, to cry, the only time he'd seen, well, actually heard, tears spurting from her eyes, to bawl like a baby and there was nothing that affected him more, her dad could have put a shotgun or a postal scale to his head, it wouldn't have had as much clout as those pathetic sobs. They tugged at his heart, those tears; she could have asked him for anything at that moment and he, he would have agreed, succumbed. Take me; he would have. Pick me up; he would have lifted. Come; he would have flown. Marry me; he would have tied the knot and flipped pizza dough forever, so rotten did he feel listening to her crying. And then, tears blown away, woman that she was, fool of a girl that she was, tragic flaw that she wore like a mark of Cain on her forehead, she caught herself, stopped dead again and, mind you, said she was *sorry*. Sorry for crying. Sorry for the tears. Sorry for breaking down. *She* was, would you believe?, *she* was sorry. After all this, she apologetic. As if she didn't want to hurt him. Which of course killed it. Out the window flew his pity for her. Whshhht, it vanished like morning mist. But when you think of it, was she really that sweet, that timid? Or was she weaving one of her masks? Did they make girls like that any more, or was that another calculated move, getting him to feel so miserable, so vulnerable with his lame excuse that he had to go to London, the London School of Economics was waiting, to feel so sorry for her that he would drop his plans to go to England and instead come to Cincinnati or Cleveland or whichever pathetic corner of the east end of town on the wrong side of the railroad tracks she lived with her boob of a dad who clerked for the postal service and her mom, a self-styled homemaker who arranged Tupperware parties to put more plastic on the table, and take her away somewhere so's both of them could be together and plan their pizza parlor future of poverty and she wouldn't have to go through that bleak crepuscular tunnel alone. She stumbled, that ominous green knapsack fell and dragged him down with it. That knapsack falls and like little bubbles, a host of girl things and contact lens potions like snowflakes or paper flakes in a mock stage scatter mock snow in slow motion on the Amexco floor and everyone else just stands there and stares while she bends down, embarrassed, to scoop up her stuff hurriedly, red in the face, absolutely humiliated, and only he, much to the chagrin of others who saw what a cute kid she was, maybe cute at first glance what with her leggy legs and chesty chest but at second and third glance rather plain in the face, he takes the initiative to help her gather her belongings which of course gets him a first edge on getting to know her, which he does by the time both of them have cashed their checks and are now standing outside, near a small arched stone bridge over a canal, watching the water, when a gondolier glides by and waves to them. He signals the gondolier to stop.

Have you ever been on a gondola? he asks her.

No. Never. I just got here. Today.

Cuanto costa, signore?

You know Italian? Oh, my God!

I minored in it at Dartmouth, he stage whispers.

Venti mille lire per quaranta cinque minuti, says the gondolier.

How much is it? Oh my Lord, it must cost a fortune.

Bene. Ma por una ora.

Per la signorina.

He's giving us a special rate. For an hour's ride. Because of the beautiful girl with me, he says.

How much! I wanna chip in.

Twenty thousand dollars.

No.

Yes. For the gondola.

You're teasing.

Yes. The twenty thousand is for the entire gondola. To buy it outright.

Her eyes flashed. With the gondolier?. . . Just kidding. . . . I'll chip in.

Forget it. My treat. In honor of your first day in Venice. The first of anything is special.

And the water was special too, sparkling in daylight as if bits of stars were floating there, the water breaking the reflections of buildings into tiny segments as if they were a cubist painting.

Not forty minutes in Venice and already in a gondola. Oh my God!

And not four hours in town and already in bed, going at it like she's never had loving before, her arms around him like she never wants to let him go, it's the first time she's ever done it, honest. That's what they all say, he teases her. It hurts her, that tease; he sees that sparkle dying in her eyes and so he holds her tighter and whispers into her ear, I believe you. I know it is. You just make love so naturally. Because it comes from my heart, she said. I fell for you, she admitted, soon as I laid eyes on you. I took one look at you standing there and I just dropped my pack. My arms grew weak, honest, just like my heart now, just like my knees. I believe if I tried to stand now, I'd fall down. It's like I swallowed a potion.

And he thinks of Cressida's famous line upon first seeing Troilus: Who gave me drinke?

Zoe. They don't make girls like you. Loving. Honest. Naïve to the core, an open Ohioan, she didn't know that you didn't tell guys a thing like that, cause it's liable to go to their heads, and end up hurting you. With the ability to love a man with every cell of her body.

"Any reason they chose the name Zoe?" he asked her.

"My dad ran out of letters."

"No! Twenty-six kids? He's four bettern'n Bach. Who preceded you? Xerxes and Yahoo?"

She smiled. She didn't get the Biblical and literary references.

"From one wife?"

"One. But seven husbands." And now Zoe began laughing.

He saw for the first time that one of her teeth was a bit crooked. No wonder she had an adorable smile. Now she didn't at all look like the demure innocent abroad like she did when she made her debut at Amexco. She was on a high now, pulling his leg, enjoying it, proud of it.

"Well done." He shook her hand formally. Even bowed a bit, Japanesely. "For a minute I almost believed you."

Zoe.

Why did I let you go?

Why?

Why?

Why?

10. Why Tommy Was in Venice

Why was he in Venice? Because it was destined that he meet Happy?

I mean, really now. The truth. No more facade.

Let the secret go.

Because of the timelessness of the city; because it never got older. Unlike Eschenbach, who needed rouge and lipstick and black hair rinse to—in the words of the obsequious barber—"to only rightfully restore what belongs to you," the city never got older. What was it that he was capturing? The agelessness of the city? No, it was something on an entirely different plane. It was guilt. There you go. Now you got it. Not for a current sin, but for a remission of the past. On occasion that deed of twenty-five years past strobed in his head like a dark light. And he would watch this noir film for the length of a dream. Did he want to seize the past and see if he could make the reel go another way and not hold its pre-determined course? Perhaps to undo that surge of Zoe's tears that played on the lids of his memory like a migraine? No, he knew that all the dreamwishing in the world could not make it vanish. For somewhere in this world a twenty-four-year-old young man was wandering about with half his genes. Or woman. That was why when he met a girl he always found out how old she was, where she came from, and if she was of that age, he backed off. No. Backed off was too tame. Withdrew. Retreated. Went into quick reverse and vanished from the scene.

It was perhaps his only mistake, moral lapse if you will. Several years back, in mid-career, he took a year off and served a year in the Peace Corp in Egypt (when asked what he did there, he always said, I worked on the DPP project, which invariably prompted the question, What's the DPP?—just the question he was waiting for, answering matter-of-factly, the Dismantle the Pyramids Project), volunteered as a coach in Washington Little League games, did other bits of odds and ends of good deeds. Helped his dad on the farm. Thought it was the right way to go. If you're kind to the earth, his father taught, the earth will be kind to you. To be kind to the earth and to the humans who populated it, although frankly the former was easier than the latter. And he was kind to Zoe, no doubt about it. Took her here and there, to cafés and concerts, to galleries and palaces, to places she'd never have gone to on her own. And he shared with her, he remembered, so many wonderful thoughts, remarks that if he had been Zoe and heard them, he'd never forget them in one hundred and one years. Things like his earliest memories of reading, marvelling that the letters didn't fall off the pages when you turned them. Or his response to a remark that Zoe once made, wishing she could fly: I quote you what Willy Shakespeare says in Act Two of *Hamlet*: Oh God, I could be sconced in a nutshell and become a Kafka of unbounded space.

He did all these nice things not in contrition, mind you, but because he happened to be—looking at himself as objectively as he could—a decent fellow. Wouldn't do wrong. Stood for older people on buses and trains, gave strangers lifts, stopped on highways to help stranded motorists, even changed a fuel filter once. He was the sort who could imagine friends and neighbors saying of him after he was done in by a freak stray bullet or felled by a cornice from some Washington landmark or killed in some lousy African conflict the President had mandated was in the American national interest and he happened to be there on assignment doing somebody's speech: He wouldn't hurt a fly. Should he eat himself because of Zoe? No. And he didn't. He observed partially the old adage: forgive and forget. He forgave himself (Zoe herself, she assured him, bore him no ill will), but he didn't forget. That is, he did forget for a while, but it would surface unexpectedly in his mind like a stain on a shirt that won't go away. You hide the shirt in the closet for a while, thinking the chemise (buttering it up with a fancy name while careful not to stain it more) will forget about its blemish, lose it somewhere in the depths of the dark closet, but when you take it out, your hopes wither—the stain hasn't disappeared. The flaw is still there. It's your hope that has vanished. And the special locus of these dark thoughts was Venice, to which he was drawn like moth to flame, man to woman, lemming to sea.

Was it possible, he asked himself, that he never married because of Zoe? Perhaps an outsider listening to the entire story and subdued by now-outmoded freudulent theories would have concluded thus. A simple open and shut case. He screwed the girl in more ways than one, and out of remorse that he never married her, he never married anyone. But Tom did not buy such simplistic reasoning. Total nonsense, he told his psychologically inept friend. I never married because I didn't find anyone to my liking. Period. It never bothered me. Honest. I had some satisfying relationships but never made the move for a permanent commitment. Had I found someone, he testifies to himself under oath, I wouldn't have thought twice about Zoe, who is probably happily married now, not giving much thought to me or to our child, if indeed there was one. Did I spend a summer in Honduras building a field hospital because of Zoe? Not on your life! Only in Newtonian physics does every action have an equal and opposite reaction. But not in real life. Don't think my whole life is a series of chain reactions from that initial implosion years ago. Buying credits, merits, from our Father who art or artn't in heaven.

Girls liked him; of that he was certain. He had a longish, rather nobly formed head, a high forehead with a little Clark Gable mustache just like his father, a decorative touch he soon got rid of. In conversation he held his head a bit a-tilt and a smidgen of an ironic gleam danced in his eyes which least one woman told him was sexy. A supercilious look, she called it, "but very sexy." He carried himself erect so that his six-foot-one seemed even taller; he had a confident, long-loped stride. When he walked into a room, or into a relationship, there was nothing tentative or self-effacing about it, unlike the way Zoe came into the American Express office; she sort of sidled in shyly, did Zoe, as if she weren't there, dropping her army green knapsack and looking with a rather timid, even frightened glance at the two rows of Americans and Europeans waiting to cash checks or pick up mail, as if she'd crashed a party where everyone knew everyone else, except her. Maybe that's why she dropped her knapsack, scattering her health and beauty aids shop, looking like a startled rabbit at the staring crowd, afraid they'd make her run the gauntlet, further calling attention to herself with her belongings scattering like marbles in a child's game, in fact one round little bottle kept spinning in the otherworldly silence of the room, attracting the attention of dozens, nay scores, of transfixed eyes; or, if adult, rolling all over the floor like billiard balls on a pool table. Another bottle just kept marching across the floor like a wound-up toy from the door to the cashier's cage and no one stopped to pick it up. It was as if her little things had been infused with a dose of magic. Zoe looked as if she wanted to be there and yet make herself invisible.

What else changed in him? His sense of time changed, subtle changes like the hormonal changes that were taking place in her, changes that bound her to him, albeit with invisible lines. He would wake up previously and take each day as it came, happy with it, optimistic about its outcome. Now he would wake up early in the morning, the middle of the night, the start of a new day, let's say Thursday, and the first thing that flew through his head was: tomorrow's Friday. Another day gone, another day will be gone; maybe tomorrow she'll have that miscarriage; maybe Friday Zoe will abort, as she had written to him that she was trying, running up stairs and taking hot baths to end the pregnancy on her own.

By now morning light swept the Piazza and the sweepers were gone. Early office workers were crisscrossing the square on their way to work in those gorgeous buildings. And he sat leaning against a pillar at the edge of the square, but unlike Samson he had no thought of bringing it down. Because he had some optimism in his life. Yes, he would see Zoe again and tell her what was in his heart. And undo the feeling he left her with as he led her around the fountain years ago at the other side of the Piazza. When she asks him why they were going round and round seven times, he tells her he once attended a wedding of a Jewish friend in Burlington and saw the bride circle seven times around the groom.

"Does that mean you're marrying me?" the utterly unsophisticated Zoe asked, totally untutored in the ways of the world.

What better way to not answer a question than with another question.

"Didn't we already consummate the marriage?"

"I suppose," she said helplessly. "But we're walking around the fountain. Then the fountain is the bride."

"The groom," he corrected her. But correcting, he now knows, is not making aright. His correcting, he now knows, had a nasty edge, a cruel bite. And he noted the sadness in her voice but said nothing in solace.

11. *The Yellow Umbrellas in the Rockefeller Center Rink*

They met by the rink in Rockefeller Center. She had not bothered him at all during her pregnancy and for that he was eternally grateful to her. He was in England, true. She knew he was at the London School of Economics; she could have found him. Could have made his life miserable; could have gotten her father or brother (if she had one) to put the screw on him. But she separated herself, went out on her own, never told her parents in Cleveland or Cincinnati and had her baby, so she said, in New York. He told her he admired her courage; he called it pluck and tenacity and hoped she wouldn't notice the cliché. When the time came to contact him, she had no difficulty finding the Manning farm in northern Vermont. How may organic dairy farmers named Manning could there be up there? She called his parents just as he was leaving London, left only her first name and phone number of a residence hotel in New York and asked, Please tell him to call me when he comes back. I'll only be here about five more weeks.

He had her phone number in his hand. It took him a month to gather up the courage to call. He could have thrown it away, but it became a paper image of her, a talisman he dared not destroy. His body told him not to call, even as his will directed his fingers at once to the dial. Scared more of the known than the unknown, he almost didn't dial the last number, but he felt he owed her at least that much.

The conversation was short and brisk. It had no subtext or undertones. She wanted to see him just once more. Her voice, the entire memory of her, created a caliginous tunnel in his soul. The tunnel grew longer and darker the more she spoke. He remembered a saying of Turgenev: the heart of another is a dark forest. Still, he knew what was driving Zoe. Just one meeting, she said on the phone. He would have to take the early train to New York. He didn't tell her this and she didn't ask. Just one meeting, she said. But it wasn't that. It couldn't be that. It was never that. When they want to see you one more time, it's never the last. It's the first of another cycle. He would resist it. He knew her; he knew her well. He wasn't going to enter that dark forest. He would see her once and that's it. Things were stable for him; he didn't want her to upset that stability. Once would be enough. Once, he owed her once. But than once no more.

The exchanges were polite. No chill in the air. How are you? How was your year in England? Are you okay? You sure? And then they arranged to meet—he could have sworn she said only five minutes, he vaguely remembered, but one couldn't blame him for being vague, for the shock of her calling him, yes, shock, for he was sure he'd never hear from her again, interfered with his hearing and thinking—by the Fifth Avenue side of the Rockefeller Center skating rink.

It was a hot day in July. He got there first. The only hint of intimacy in their talk the other night was: Will you recognize me? Of course, he said gently. I'd recognize you anywhere. He didn't ask her what she would wear, figured she chose Rockefeller Center because she knew the area. He paced up and down the sidewalk, looking down at the rink, now a garden café. He remembered the winter scene when skaters went round and round to sound of sweet waltzes and middlebrow music. Now, in July, tables with bright yellow umbrellas were spread on the rink, and waiters seemed to glide on the shiny parquet. It made a beautiful picture looking down on the yellow umbrellas and no music, no music at all, not in the rink, not in his heart. Then spotted her, his heart pounding, all the yellow umbrellas drumming in his tight ribcage, coming up the walk from Fifth Avenue in a white skirt and peach-colored short-sleeved blouse. She looked good. She'd even gotten prettier. What, he wondered, had she done to herself? Her face thinner, more mature. Gone that lost-in-Venice innocence of a year ago as she came through the Amexco door and spilled the contents of her fairytale forest green knapsack all over the floor and he glides over like a gondola to help her gather her things.

He didn't shake her hand. He wanted to hold her shoulders, but his hands were lead weights on his thighs.

"Hi," she said softly, looking up at him.

He wasn't slouching but he felt he was slouching. They looked at each other for a long time before she spoke, and during that moment had a wind come he would have fallen, although during that tormented moment he persuaded himself that a look of understanding, even forgiveness, warmed in her eyes. That and the rabbit timidity he saw in her eyes made him stand straight. He felt they were on a see-saw and he was high on it.

"I just wanted to see you once more," she said softly. "I didn't want that vague image to fade away. Do you understand?"

"Yes," he whispered.

"Do you really?" And with that subtly scolding phrase she shifted the balance now and moved high on the see-saw. "Do you really understand that I had to, I just had to make face-to-face contact with you. To convince myself you're real. That that week last year in Venice wasn't just a dream. That you weren't just a dream. It's important to me. I don't know if it's important to you, but it's important to me. It's important to me."

"You look wonderful." He looked at her breasts, even fuller now. Perhaps she was still nursing.

Zoe smiled a sad smile. "What are you doing now? Do you mind if I ask you?"

Apologetic again. Timid again. Pavid as usual. She could not remain high on that see-saw for long. She didn't realize she had the right to ask, to demand anything of him. Anything at all.

"No. I don't mind."

"Your year in London. Was it good?"

"Very good. A year at school and with the MP the second semester, interning and helping him write his speeches. We got along well, the Brit and the Yank. I think he rather liked me."

"It's no wonder," she said, no hint of irony in her voice.

"And toward the end of the year, the MP introduced me to a Washington lawyer friend of his. You know, the OBN. . . ."

"What's that?"

"The Old Boys' Network . . . and before you know it, I got a temporary job in the economics lobbying section of his office. Until, he promised me, something better came along."

"I still don't know what you do . . . what is it exactly that you do? I mean, what's your job?"

"I hang around hotel lobbies."

She laughed the old, familiar laugh. Her head thrown back once, the eyes up for a moment, and then the laugh turning into a smile.

What he didn't tell her was that after three weeks, the lawyer, who knew Bobby Kennedy, recommended him for an opening on

Kennedy's staff, where he had just started a week ago. In short, at twenty-three, he was working for Kennedy, as an assistant to his chief speech writer. He didn't tell Zoe this because he didn't want to brag. He didn't want to give her an opening to say, I was too small-time, too insignificant for you. You're gonna be big time.

Are you proud of me? he wanted to ask her, because he wanted her to be proud of him. All his work this past year was done so she should be proud of him. But that would have been too intimate, too inappropriate, under the circumstances. But that little personal thought made him want to hug her, to show he still felt something for her—mostly sorry. But he restrained himself on that too.

"I'm proud of you," Zoe said, preternatural as a witch, and the remark, so it seemed to him, brought tears to her eyes. He wondered if her eyes would cloud over. In a film, a line like that would prompt wet lashes and pinched nostrils and choked back tears. But he couldn't see if there were tears in her eyes. Perhaps because his own eyes misted over. Or perhaps they didn't. But he knew that all this chit-chat was a charade. They were talking around and around. A phantom carousel, without music, sans ring. The thing they should have talked about dangled on a rope, letters all jumbled on a gray placard before his eyes.

"I always was, remember?"

Remember? That word for him was the madeleine dipped into the milk tea. It caused the floodgates of his vulnerable memory to rupture. *Remember?* How could he forget? He remembered everything. Forgot nothing.

12. Perpetuo Mobile of Memories

His whole life now, he mused, was one long remember. Remember that jewel box, Teatro La Fenice, with its delicate floral hand-painted panels in the six tiers of balconies? Remember how the people gazing down looked as if they were pictures in frames? Remember the simple grandeur of that Venetian chandelier? And there was that girl who sat in the rightmost parterre all by herself and faced the audience and I imagined it was you up there and at intermission I would go up and introduce myself and then open the lid of the jewel box to see the gems of the sky, for we were closed in by the music that night, the Beethoven quartet transported us to a different world, and as we walked along the Strada Grande, enjoying the clacking of an occasional heel, suddenly on our left a palazzo was bathed in a blaze of light, the Ca Pesaro on the Grand Canal.

And remember we walked on Via Garibaldi, the widest street in Venice, not far from the Piazza? It was early and no one, no one at all was out, just the two of us, and we didn't want to speak lest we wake someone and spoil the privacy of our owning the Venetian street, having it all to ourselves, my sneakers made no sound but your sandals did, and except for the tolling of the church bells, that was the only sound on the street that morning, even the tourist pigeons of San Marco don't venture into the real Venetian streets. We peeked into one calle after another, marvelled at the gorgeous pastel colors, green offsetting gold, russet shutters on a muted ochre wall, saw the laundry, the ubiquitous laundry that the tourist board hangs out for effect, saw the sheets and pants hanging between the narrow walls, and at the end of one calle came upon the water and one of the hundreds of narrow canals and a shaft of sunlight was shining on the water and on the narrow stone bridge.

"Remember," he said aloud now, "those divine acoustics at the Scuola San Stefano, the all-Vivaldi concert the night of the first day we met. When the music began, soaring up to heaven, or maybe descending from it, we looked at each other. We didn't have to say a word. The music spoke for us. The sounds of that Vivaldi seemed to hang in the air. Remember? Remember that night?"

She did.

I never felt anything like that magic before. Or since.

Stop it, she said. Stop.

He did.

Saw the tears in her eyes. First time he saw tears in her eyes. No longer ambiguous or imagined. Was she crying for the baby she had had all alone? Or for losing him? Or were those tears tears of sadness for the sad saga of both of them, of the three of them? He looked down at the pavement of Rockefeller Center, glittering with the fallen notes of that Vivaldi.

It was a very short piece, he said, trying to divert her. About five minutes. It was over quicker than we thought. Nothing lasts forever. I guess heaven is fleeting too.

Just one more thing, please, he said.

She looked down, sadly, he thought, with a touch of drama. He wondered if she'd learned that look from a movie. As if to say, he's hopeless. There's no stopping him. There should be a close-up now, he thought, as she slowly raised her head and eyes and nodded.

Would he have stopped had she said no?

Remember they played the first Vivaldi piece again as an encore.

She did.

And when they finished the opening piece, I whispered in your ear during the enthusiastic applause: I'll bet they play it again as an encore.

They did, she said.

For awhile, neither said a word. Like their lives, they stared in different directions.

You said, Zoe remembered, that that Vivaldi was a moving piece. Then you explained, and I still don't know if you were joking or not, that it made you move in your seat, move your head, move your neck, your arms, your body. The music propels you, you said. That's what a moving piece means, you said.

I wasn't joking, he said. Then added slowly, not noticing the noonday crowd of strollers and tourists making paths around them as if they were the center of a small universe, From the first few notes we both felt we were in the presence of magic. That the music was saying for both of us what we felt but could not say.

He looked at her, but her face was a blank.

Was it the music, he wondered, that drew them together? The magic of the city, the romance of the romance of Venice? Or was it something between them external to the magic veil that the city wrapped around itself?

Now he couldn't stop although Zoe had ordered him to stop.

"Remember how I wanted to have a picture of me standing on the balcony of the Ca D'Oro and you went out with my camera, boarded a vaporetto at the Ca D'Oro station and I waited there on the balcony, like Juliet, for a half hour until you changed vaporettos and took the boat back and snapped a picture of me from the boat?"

Because you asked me to.

True. But it was still very nice of you.

Because I'm nice.

I never said you weren't. Thinking: I understand the dig, which he swallowed in silence.

Because if you like someone, you do nice things for him.

Enough, he thought he heard her say. Now it's really enough.

But he was a rock tumbling downhill.

Remember how in the Hotel Danieli, when for a lark we went in to inquire about rates, when the bellhop left us alone, how in the hallway of the suite we opened up the old inside window made of thick circles of glass that stopped prying eyes? You called it ashtray glass and I called it the *occhiale* for giants and we looked down four flights into the lobby below. Tapestries on the walls, Persian carpets on the parquet floors. Antique furniture everywhere. Marble staircase in the lobby that for centuries has been known as the golden staircase which I escorted you on, making believe you were a princess, which you are.

Maybe he was remembering so much, he remembered thinking, because it postponed the essential. The thing they should have talked about wasn't talked about. But it would come. It would. Inevitable, like gravity and sunset.

He wasn't wrong. As if reading his mind again, a moment later she asked him, and she wasn't shy now. She looked directly into his eyes.

"Don't you want to know if it was a boy or a girl?"

13. *The Eternal Question*

"No," Tom said firmly. He was sure it was a boy. His sort, strong, masculine, testosterone-driven, confident, always created male children. There had been boys in his family for generations. Even further back than that. He came from a long line of male Mannings. His father, grandfather, great-grandfather, were all Vermont men. The first syllable of his name, Mann, meant man. So why should the line end with him?

"All right," she said, weak now, taken aback. The hard edge of that definitive "no" astonished her. He saw something, didn't know what, color, cells, mood, falling on her face.

A church bell pealed. Maybe someone was getting married in St. Patrick's Cathedral. The notes carried. Zoe heard them, caught them, cast them away.

Tom looked down at the scattered notes on the pavement, lying in a discord of their own. Just a year ago, that concert with Zoe. He could still see the hall's magnificent coffered ceiling without even closing his eyes. A year ago he had wondered if the notes that floated up stayed there. But now instead of notes he saw the alternating glint of glass and shiny black obsidian fragments of the sidewalk. Boy, girl, they twinkled at him, boy, girl, and he wondered but didn't want to wonder, willed himself, fists tightened, to block his mind from wondering, but with those tears in her eyes Zoe was again manipulating him in her own sweet innocent harmless-looking way, making him feel awful with that brisk and emphatic "Stop it," when he just sought to hold on to a memory of her that she just as soon would have let melt away.

In Venice, she had told him she had a dream that they were on a canoe on a fast-moving river and that she fell off and he reached for her but a space of air separated her hand from his like the finger of Adam from God on the Sistine Chapel ceiling and the canoe moved one way and she another until the space between them grew larger and she was watching this as if she were a cinematographer filming the scene, watching the gap between them growing so vast that he and the canoe were at the extreme left of the screen and she on the extreme right, sinking, and the expanse of water filling the vast screen but what was worse she wasn't feeling she was drowning as much as she was being abandoned, left to drown, because he made no move to get out of the canoe. But the truth of the matter was that it wasn't her dream at all, but his.

Not only was there silence between them now but a stasis as if they were frozen expressionless on a photograph, two strangers with nothing but history between them.

He didn't know what to do now? Invite her for a drink? Lunch? Take a stroll? He had absolutely no feelings for her. He loved memories, the cellophane around reality. Felt only that he had to get away. No, there *was* a feeling. Same as before.

Pity.

"I want to ask you one question. Can I?" Zoe said.

He didn't want her to ask one question, he thinks. Not even two. I'm uncomfortable speaking to you. Forgive me. I'm sorry for what I have done. I hope you can get on with your life as you seem to have done. Looking good. Nicely dressed. Wish you well. Goodbye.

He looked at Zoe. There was an emptiness in her and he had put that emptiness into her.

"Okay," he said, surprised at the equanimity of his voice.

"Did you love me?"

Did, she says; not do, says she. Finally. This. *This* was the reason she'd asked to meet him. It took her a while, but she finally gets it out.

I'll answer that, he says. I will. But first let me ask *you* a question:

"Why didn't you shout, scream, curse, throw things? Why didn't you call me a rat, son of a bitch, bastard, for deserting you? Why didn't you say you'll tell your parents, my parents? That you'd call the police. The vice squad. Decent people don't do things like what I did."

"Would it have helped?" she said.

"Maybe. . . . In fact, sure."

"You'd have married me," she said flatly. But the music, the phrasing of her voice sang faintly with sarcasm. Incredulity was the anagram of her words.

"Something like that," he said. But instead I wished you away. I hoped you'd disappear. Vanish. That one day I'd wake up and you wouldn't be there. That the problem would just go away on its own.

You wanted me dead, right? he heard her say, although she looked at him silently, with those large, hurt, lamb eyes. You know, once I dreamt that a serpent ate my heart while you were watching and you just stood there and did nothing. It's a story, he thought, right out of the folktales. A pre-packaged dream. Yes, don't deny it, admit it, think about it. You wanted me out of your life. Anything than having the embarrassment of a knocked-up girlfriend hanging around, upsetting your life. Because you wanted to go to London at all costs. Your career came first. And I was suddenly in the way. In the family way, he corrected. Oh, how you would have wanted me to abort on my own. Have a miscarriage. Have some magic treatment that would make me vanish and no one would see me any more. But no, I took a deep breath and, for you—for *you*, you louse—I did it, stupidly on my own. To save *your* skin. *Your* neck. *Your* honor. And now you don't even want to know if it was a boy or a girl. Because by not knowing you can still pretend, still fool yourself that it doesn't exist.

I knew it was a boy. I just knew it.

She didn't confirm or deny. Give a sad smile or cry.

Why don't you answer me? she shouted. Say a word. Say something.

She began pounding him on the chest, almost a parody of a weak woman hitting a strong man, but rhythmically, without stopping. And she did this in broad daylight, in Rockefeller Center, in front of throngs of people who walked around them and admired the big yellow umbrellas of the skating rink café. Well? Say something. Anything. Say I'm sorry. Say I'm glad. Say I did it. Say I was stupid. Say something for God's sake. Anything is better than that stubborn, malicious, unfeeling silence of yours.

Why didn't you complain? he said. You took everything I did with such martyr-like silence. It's unheard of. You could have blackmailed me. Ruined me. Taken advantage of me. But like a saint you took it all.

"Because I loved you," Zoe said. "Did you love me?"

And now she doesn't even look angry, he thinks. Now she looks serene. Why couldn't she sustain her anger? He wanted her furious. What was wrong with Zoe? She didn't do anything normally. Zoe had a screw loose. And it was all the fault of her name. If she wouldn't have had such an oddball, Z-weighted name, she would have been like everyone else.

Do you have any idea of the depth of love? Zoe asks him. How much one person can love another? She spoke looking down at the sidewalk and he felt he was one of the glinting little diamonds on the concrete, looking up at her as if she were a gigantic genie with the blue sky arching above her head. It's only because I loved you so much, so much, that I didn't want to stand in your way, break up your plans, even though you broke mine. That's how much I loved you, did you, she said quickly without so much as a slight insuck of breath, love me?

He heard the words she said but in his ears they rang like foreign tongue, words of an aria in a lingua nicht comprende.

Remember, he asked her silently, we climbed to the top of the Bell Tower? It was not guarded that festive night and there was no one there, for everyone was down below celebrating and we saw all of Venice lit up before us and we made love. You protested at first that people would see us and I said we can see them but they can't see us, for everyone is down below, no one would think of coming up here, and between the two of us we saw all of Venice, you the lagoon with a chain of candlelit gondolas and the Grand Canal full of pleasure boats and gondolas adorned with lights and kerosene lamps and torches and fireworks, even though you said your eyes were closed, and me the Piazza San Marco all lit up and people dancing in the Square and on the rooftops of Venice. Then everything was bright, an explosion of light, for at midnight they light the flares and turn up the lamps on the gondolas and everything else that floats and the torches that the revelers carry, it surprised us, for night turned into day. You said, Did we fall asleep? It must be morning already for the lights were so bright. That's when the baby was made. Up there, in the Bell Tower. That Festa night.

"Do you still have those absurd ideas?" Zoe asked suddenly.

He knew he still owed her an answer to that other question. Perhaps she was giving him time.

"Like what?"

"Speculation, philosophic, on things that don't lend themselves to it."

"Give an example."

Zoe thought a while. "Like once, when we took that day trip to Vicenza, we were walking along a field and saw part of a fence...."

"You mean that ten-foot gridded trellis on the side of a patch of meadow, a fence that led nowhere?"

"Yes. Remember? I wondered what in heaven's name it was doing there, that trellis that let no one in and kept no one out. It was probably the start of extensive fencing that stopped mysteriously. And you suggested it was there, in Palladio's backyard, to prompt philosophical speculation as to its existence and trigger introspection where there had been none before."

He was impressed with her memory, phrasing, vocabulary. Pregnancy had improved her. He guessed it was his infusion into her that did it.

"And then *you* said that the purpose of the gate was then served," Tom told her.

"So you do remember."

"Now I do." And he smiled. But that smile embarrassed him because he saw the pain on Zoe's face behind the placidity of her expression. The pain that he had caused. Or was it pain he imputed to her? Maybe she had risen to a state beyond pain, a state where only pity for him existed. He'd had enough. He wanted to get away quickly.

From her.

From the baby they supposedly shared that she no longer (so he assumed) had and he never wanted.

But how does one, can one, could one say goodbye under such circumstances? Was there a protocol for separating from one's short term lover whom one had put in the family way and done nothing for? Does the *Common Book of Etiquette* deal with it in Chapter III?

Tom closed his eyes for a moment, speculating again. How can someone be in two places at the same time? In front of the skating rink and yet six blocks away in front of the New York Public Library, riding one of the lions to freedom.

But Zoe seemed to want to hold on. He was suspicious of her agenda. Five minutes, in women's math, could very well become five years.

"Did you ever develop that anti-trunk theft device of yours?"

He laughed. "Anti-*theft* trunk device. . . . No."

"Why? Laziness? Indolence? Inertia?"

"*Au contraire.* I had trouble with the prototype."

"You actually made a prototype? Then I apologize."

He nods. He remembered telling her about it on one of the islands near Venice. "You know where I told it to you. On one of those islands, what's that name again, they sound so much alike, one specializes in lace, Bolero, that's it, and the other in glass, um, yeah, Sombrero, that's where I told it to you, while we were walking in Bolero."

He had had enough of trunk thefts in New York. He wanted to put a sign on his trunk: I gave at the office. But how would that satisfy him if the hoods picked and broke his lock and stole everything in sight, whether usable resalable or not? So he got an idea for a device that would activate, viciously, aggressively, if someone picked open the trunk lock. As soon as the trunk door was raised and the crook bent forward to grab something, a spring would release a boxing glove that would smash into the goon's face. And as he reeled backwards, two grappling hooks would seize his arms and drag him forward and down into the trunk. The door would then drop over the two flailing and kicking legs until the cops came.

"But something didn't work."

"You had trouble with it."

"Yes. That stupid thing couldn't tell friend from foe. It was like out of a Three Stooges comedy. In Washington once after a concert I wanted to check if my packages were still in the trunk. I went to my car, forgot to override the alarm, lifted the trunk door and saw that gloved fist coming. First thing that flashed through my mind was me telling it, Stop, it's me! But go talk to a spring. No feelings, no loyalty, no pity. Instead, it punched me in the face. Then the two hooks pulled me into the trunk. The lid closed, my shins were bruised and, to add insult to injury, I was arrested for forcible entry into a parked vehicle. Mine!"

Zoe laughed so hard he again felt bad for her.

"But what was worse, when I tried to sue myself, my lawyer suggested that we settle out of court."

Forced mirth, forced meeting. For it was Zoe who wanted it, insisted on it, guilted him into it by saying mildly, You owe me at least that much, a tender coercion which to her credit she did not repeat. Not even a hint of it. The hundreds of passersby, had one of them stood nearby casually and listened, would have thought that this couple was hitting it off splendidly. But now Tom stopped to wonder if her friendliness wasn't also a kind of coercion, a flirtatiousness to draw him back to her. Again, she didn't want to let him go. Again she was hooking him like she did last year with that pregnancy ploy. But as he wondered how he could graciously withdraw (for he could say, I'll be back in a minute, I have to go to the bathroom, and never return, as he and a pal had once done some years back when stuck with two awful gold-digging broads they'd picked up), it was she who, business-like, as if a mask had been drawn over her, proclaimed assertively: "You must be going back to what you're doing and I must too." Just as he was starting to warm to her again.

He was about to look at his watch, then decided it would be too insensitive. He couldn't tell if they had been talking five minutes or fifty.

"Some five minutes," he said anyway.

Zoe laughed. When she laughed, he saw the look in her eye that he had seen in Venice. She couldn't control it; she could hide it but not stop it. She's still in love with me, he thought. Her eyes melting, soft, shining with adoration, a moment of ecstasy glowing there as she shared laughter with him. But then, as if catching himself, taking hold of the reins, the cloud covered the sun.

Her question pressed at his soul like a thumb in the eye.

15. When You Take a Girl to a Luxury Hotel
Is That a Sign of Love?

Was his wanting to take her to the Danieli, was that love?

Zoe and he had walked past the Danieli a few times, admiring its palatial façade (he told her it had appeared in 16th century paintings) and Grand Canal location, around the corner from Piazza San Marco, and a short walk from the Bridge of Sighs. Once they got up enough nerve to walk in, they were amazed by the aura of wealth it exuded. The marble staircase, the concierges in morning coats. May I help you? a clerk asked him. He looked at their jeans, but his face registered no disdain.

"We'd like to see a room."

"Canal view or courtyard?"

"Canal, please."

The clerk called a bellhop who asked them to be seated for a moment while he checked if the room was made. They sat in the lobby in deep easy chairs. A huge oil painting of Venice was above them. People sipped cocktails. Unseen, a pianist was playing.

"I don't believe you're doing this," Zoe whispered.

"Why not? I'm a potential customer."

The bellhop showed them a room on the second floor with two huge canopy beds, brocaded drapery and a silver bowl in the shape of a gondola piled with fruits. They stepped out into the little balcony, floating on air, floating in Venice.

"How much is this room?"

"I don't know, sir. Reception will tell you."

He remembered that then, in the mid 60's, 1967 to be exact, it was $200 a night.

The question, Do you love me? bobbed like an empty gondola in his mind. It echoed with circles of the past. He recalls he is a little boy and his mother asks him, Do you love me? Do you love your mommy?

Zoe was waiting. Did you love me?

"Shall I call you something nice?" he tells Zoe, deflecting for another moment her question, but knowing he'd have to answer it. He wonders if she remembers the allusion. She smiles, for she had once asked him:

"Why don't you call me something nice for a change, like vivacious or perspicacious?"

"I only call you," Tom teased her, "names that you can spell."

Her smile did not blow the question away. Her question hung in the air like a black cloud that would not budge. It also hung on his neck, a twenty-pound weight.

"Did you love me?" she asked again. "Why don't you answer me?" But it cost her, that question. It cost her, riding that question on the rocky road of let's pretend love. Every time she said it, another pint of lifeblood drained out of her. She looked like a wounded animal before the kill, he saw. If ever there was an auspicious time for telling the truth it wasn't now.

Still, he couldn't bring himself to lie. It wasn't right. Cheers from the audience on one side of his brain. But if I tell the truth, I'll hurt her. Tumultuous standing ovation from the crowd on the other side of the cranium stadium. His skin, his very hair, prickles with electricity, for at bottom, like the French philosopher Levinas maintains, we are still one person. One sack of bones, despite our antinomial thoughts, our polarized attitudes, our schizoid stances.

If ever there was a time to lie it was now. If ever it was a good and righteous deed to bend the truth like cheap tin, like kids' clay, it was now. If ever a lie was needed, was inexorable in its pull, it was now. If ever a lie was medicinal, a balm, a salve, a palliative, it was now. Now. Now. Now.

"Did you love me?" she asked again.

He smiled at her. And why the past tense, pessimist? he was about to say, then realized that words like that were worse than the truth.

He told her:

"*Fosti il mio primo amore e l'ultimo sarai.*"

"Which means?"

"You were my first love, you'll be my last. But I told you that, in these very words, in Venice last year. You forgot?"

He could see the breath, the breath of joy, slowly exhaling.

"I'm glad," she said, and a ray of warmth beamed through her officious demeanor.

"It's from *Idomineo*, by Mozart."

"Really?"

He nodded slowly, closing his eyes. Again he wanted to clasp her shoulders but refrained.

"*Ch'io mi scordi di te?*" he asked her.

"What's this Italian thing?"

"I'm inspired. Memories of Italy. It means: You want me to forget you?"

Wisely she replied, "That's up to you. One of us maybe doesn't want to remember, but one of us can't forget."

Pain makes a woman articulate; pain is a stone on which razor keen wit is honed.

Nobody else could see it, he knew, not a soul among the thousands who milled around the midtown area, but he saw it, he heard it, he knew there was an asp hiding between the letters of those beneficent words.

"And furthermore:

"*Tu virginum corona, tu nobis pacem dona, tu consolare affectus unde suspirat cor. . . .* From Mozart's *Exultate Jubilate.* Thou crown of virgins, give us peace, and calm the passions which trouble our heart."

"Amen," said Zoe. Her eyes glowed and she smiled. But he saw that her "Amen" had a finality to it, like the end of a prayer. In his mind's eye he took her hands and pressed her close. He put his lips to her neck and muttered, I'm sorry. You're special. I never met a girl like you—

Now it was his turn to hold on to the string. An idea he thought he'd share with her. *That* would be a graceful exit, if anything, for it would combine exit without letting go.

So just as she was about to turn, he told her what he had prepared long before the Rockefeller Center meeting.

"Wait! I have an interesting idea for you, for us. Something very unusual. Wanna hear?"

She stopped. "Okay."

Why doesn't she say, I don't want to hear a thing. I want to leave now. What's wrong with her?

"I once heard, maybe I read, about a young couple, not married, who are splitting up, who make a promise to each other to meet in twenty-five years at a certain place, time and date."

She looked blankly at him. Then said, "So?"

She said "So?", not "no." Feeling that he had the advantage, he pressed on. "Like out of a classic fable we promise each other,

All right, we, say, we're separating now, but in twenty-four— "

"Twenty-four? I thought you said twenty-five. . .?"

"I'll explain in a minute. . . . In twenty-four years I'll meet you, is what he says to her, and she replies: I'll try. No matter where I am, what I'm doing, who I am, I'll come. Me too, he says, and we'll meet and be surprised that both of us acted on our plan of years ago and actually came, and the joy of fulfilling that promise will be as great as the actual meeting. I can see us now, me tall and handsome with a touch of gray at the temples, mature and successful, and you still looking as you do now, not a day older. She listens to what he has to say and smiles at his foolishness, perhaps at the silly dream of meeting so many years later, a geste direct from storybooks or the stuff from which films are made.... What do you say?"

"Well, you've already written the scenario."

"Still, it's your choice."

"Is it really?"

"Of course it is," he said softly.

Zoe thought for a minute, looked up at the skyscraper as if high stories or heaven would provide guidance. Now that he had articulated it, he realized what a stupid, unattainable idea this was; still, there was enough in it to make it fascinating, something to look forward to. He observed that he wasn't rooting one way or another for her decision. Whatever she said would be fine.

You've got to be joking, she could say sullenly. Why should I meet *you*?

"In twenty-five years you say."

Was she calculating what year it would be?

"Yes. But from last year. Twenty-five years from our first meeting. That makes it 1992. Or, twenty-four from this year."

"Where?"

His heart thumped, skittered, metronomed presto. "Where?" she said, not no.

"Well, that might be a problem," he said. "But it has to be Venice."

"On the Festa del Redentore?"

"Of course."

"That's a big trip."

"If you show up, I'll reimburse your air fare."

"And if I don't?"

"If you don't, I won't. . . . "

"Where do we meet?"

"By the fountain."

"Why not Amexco?"

"Because it may not be there then. Offices come and go but the fountain at the Piazza San Marco will be there. And anyway, maybe my knees won't be so good by then and I don't want to bend down and pick up your drugstore, your—to make a railroad pun—your rolling stock."

Zoe smiled again, perhaps remembering the funny way they met. And recited the details as if she wanted to impress them on her memory.

"The place, Venice. The locale, the fountain in Piazza San Marco. The date, third Sunday in July, Festa del Redentore. The year, 1992. Let's see, mmm, we left out only one thing."

"What's that?" and an immediate fear waved over him, a pain as transparent as water. She's going to say: Can I bring our child?

"How will I know you'll be there?" said Zoe.

"Does the sun rise, do the rains fall, the seasons change? I'll be there."

"Wait a minute! My God! What time?"

He put a finger to his lips. "Let's see. 10:30 at night. That's when the crowds thin out, I noticed, to go to eat, and then they regather for midnight."

"The time: 10:30 p.m. and you reimburse airfare."

"Yes. If you show up."

"It's a date," Zoe said.

"No. It's a day. Not a date. The Festa is not on a specific date. . ." Zoe was nodding.

". . . it's the 3rd Sunday in July. So it's not a date but a day."

"I mean a date date."

"Yes, I know. But you know what I mean."

"Your mind is still convoluted. Even after spending a year with the English."

"Like Hamlet, one goes to England to regain one's wits, not lose them."

She liked that and flashed him a warm smile.

"Wait," he said. "There's another thing. What if one of us is late? Let's see . . . ummm!"

And he began calculating. What would be a proper wait after a twenty-four-year separation? If you plan to meet someone by the fountain in Lincoln Center and your friend is late, you wait thirty-forty minutes, maybe even into the second act. Who knows? A subway could have been stuck in the tunnel, a flat if coming by car. So how long do you wait if you travel three thousand miles one way after a twenty-five-year wait? Two hours? Three? A week? A year? Glued in perpetuity to the fountain, becoming a new statue by Bernini, or posing like a mime in a clown-freeze position till she shows up?

"How about an hour? Even ninety minutes," he proposed. "After all it's been a long wait. You gotta give it some proportion."

"Ninety minutes sounds good to me," Zoe said.

"Wonderful. This will give me something to look forward to. . . . To live for," he said with feeling, but she was too timid or too stupid or maybe too smart to rebut: Why wait that long? We can be together now?

"Okay," Zoe said.

"Don't forget," he said, "it's twenty-five years from the last year. The year we met. Not twenty-five years from now."

"Who knows where we'll be? Will we be alive?"

"Of course we will. Hale and hearty and alive and meeting in

Venice on the Festa in 1992."

He thought of bending over and giving her a kiss on the cheek, if not on the eye, but then thought it over. It might appear solicitous, forced, even hypocritical. He didn't even shake her hand.

"And I'll have a surprise for you," he said, hoping he hadn't given her an opening to say: And I'll have one for you.

By that sudden stiffening of her face, shoulders and back, he knew she had heard him.

And I'll have one for you, he heard in the echo chamber of his mind, which loved balances, adored correspondences.

"Goodbye, Tommy."

He looked for music in her voice. Couldn't find music in her voice. Was dirge music?

"That's the first time you said my name all this time," he said.

Pro-forma duty done, five minutes proffered, it was time to leave.

Then Zoe opened her pocketbook, gave him a little paper-wrapped packet, and with a sad little smile— "and you didn't say mine once" —turned quickly, walked away, and melted into the noonday crowd. Vanished. As if she'd never been. Disappeared completely. Was it forever? Tom wondered. Or just twenty-four years. He started after her. But was too late. She was gone. Where can I reach you? he wanted to ask. To remind you. To confirm our date. Too bad he hadn't asked. Too bad he was too dumb to handle this unique date with intelligence. At a corner phone booth he called the number she'd given his parents. The hotel he had called a few days earlier. The receptionist said she had already checked out.

Later, on the subway, he opened her gift. What a sweetheart! She remembered he loved Tolstoy. A story collection: *God Sees the Truth but Waits.*

And he, he now regretted that he had brought her nothing.

Except heartache.

17. I'd Love To See a Picture

He wanted to be sympathetic; he tried to gather from the air the sympathy that floated in the world and wave it into himself. An outsider, seeing him moving both his arms, might have thought he was hot and trying to cool off. Yes, he wanted to be sympathetic. But yet, but yet, but yet he could not suppress some objective thoughts.

Had he ever seen her belly? And if he had, who says it couldn't have been faked, like they do in films and theater, with pillows, sponges, Styrofoam. Did he ever see the alleged baby? Indeed, what proof was there, besides her word, that she was and indeed had been pregnant and had had a child? Reasonable doubt of reasonable men could well conclude that it all might have been an elaborate ploy, plot, play—note how all the words are related to drama—to hook him into marriage. And that's precisely why she didn't pursue him with the intensity that other mothers-to-be pursued their up-knockers. The very fact that she left him alone showed she was bluffing. Then why did she go through with her visit to Rockefeller Center, to which she'd summoned him? Why did she want it? Simple. To continue the bluff she had begun about a year before. By then the charade had taken on a life of its own and the show was by now long-running. Who knows, if Zoe had had more zeal, she could have asked for birthday gifts for this non-existent child. And what if—just *what if* he'd have said to her, when he met her at Rockefeller Center, Can I see a picture of the baby? I'd love to see a picture. What if he'd said that? Only a triplet of clichés that, like the Italians say, trip over one's tongue, could adequately portray her reaction to his innocent question: Can I see a snapshot of the baby? *That* would have floored her, sent her for a loop, pulled the rug from under her. He could have been sarcastic, and said: Yes, let's see a picture of that phantom kid. . . . I'll eat the snapshot if you can show me one. But, regrettably, he didn't do that. Couldn't do that. Because on the one in a hundred chance that she was on the mark, it wouldn't be fair to add insult to injury and claim she was lying when she wasn't lying at all and his was the peccadillo in abandoning her. *That* much sensitivity he did have. His mouth would never have articulated his innermost thoughts.

Thinking of Zoe, he felt sorry for a life lost, a life he too had lost, and wondered if that twenty-four-year date were not a last ditch effort on his part to re-right the past, restore the loss, reclaim some hope. He wondered if that meeting with her on Festa night twenty-four years from now was his way of looking for a moment of salvation in a stupid past that could have been the future he might have shaped with both hands—instead of using them to breeze some sympathy into his lungs—had he not shattered it with malice aforethought.

END

1. Who Is More Sarcastic?

"Good news," Happy told him with a broad smile. "I thought I'd be stuck at the pensione with the little girl on Festa night—"

His stomach sinking, a slow revolution of electric shocks tunneling through his limbs, turning skin to leather and nerves to ash. He urged his brain to quickly churn up ideas, come up with a quick response.

"—but my bosses are taking the girl out that night for the festivities. . . ."

You probably put her up to it, he didn't say.

". . . so I'll be able to join you."

He didn't quite know how to break the news to her. He had no ideas, no diversionary tactics. So he told her directly, even while he held her. Saying softly:

"I won't be able to spend Festa night with you. I have a longstanding appointment, I think I told you that."

She stared at him. Said nothing. Her face spoke for her lips.

"It was arranged a long time ago, even before I met you," he said, annoyed for attempting to exculpate himself.

He felt her stiffening. The color of her face changed. The good mood in the room grew chill. Her hand on his chest became heavier, as if by withdrawing her love, by sucking it back into herself, that hand became a dead limb instead of an extension of her affection. The music in the room, whatever music there had been, it wasn't the same. Her notes and his clashed, like C and B struck together.

"Fer goodness sake," he complained. "It's just one evening. It's been planned long ago. I told you. Even before I met you."

But she steamrolled on, righteous indignation in tandem with her wrath. "And now I'm in the way and have to be disposed of."

"I'm not disposing of you but, yes, you'll be in the way."

She looked at him, disarmed perhaps by his frankness, then changed her tune. "And I've been looking forward to spending the Festa night with you. . . ." Now wheedling and whining: "I've read all about it, you told me about it, and now—zilch."

That idiotic last word got him. It summed up for him all her negative intellection, the entire ambience of her Albany grease-joint dad and half-gypsy mom heritage—zilch.

"Where are you meeting her?" Happy demanded.

"Who says it's a her?"

"Me. I know it's a her. It's written all over your face. Tell me I'm wrong."

"Of course you're wrong."

She left the room, slammed the door hard. He didn't budge. He knew she'd come back. He didn't hear her walking down the stairs. She was probably waiting for him to rush to the door. But he restrained himself, waiting for her to come back. As he heard her approaching the door, he jumped up and opened it, a big smile on his face. He spread his arms in welcome.

"*Ch'io mi scordi di te,*" he said.

"Which means?"

"Do you want me to forget you?"

"No," she said with a petulant smile. "But you don't love me."

"*Au contraire,* he tells the wench in French. *Fosti il mio primo amore e l'ultimo sarai.*"

"Really?"

"Yes."

"Do you swear?"

"I don't swear, but I heartfully affirm."

"Now translate. I didn't understand a word of it."

He couldn't help laughing. "You're cute. It means, You were my first love and you'll be my last.... And like Mozart says in *Exultate Jubilate*: *Tu virginum corona, tu nobis pacem dona, tu consolare affectus unde suspirat cor. . . .*"

"I heard a virgin in there. . . ."

"Meaning: Thou crown of virgins, give us peace, and calm passions which trouble our heart."

She looked at him, calmed, but still troubled. He saw she didn't know what to make of his words, whether to consider them bluff or truth.

"There are certain passions I don't want calmed," she said.

True, she was 50% grease joint and 50% gypsy. But her body was 100% divine.

"I came back," she said, "but it's not peace. Just truce."

"Truce with you is better than peace with anyone else."

"But I'm still annoyed. I can't help it. I can't hide it...." Her eyes narrowed. "Now I get it. You're married," she spat out suddenly. "And I've been your toy. I just figured it out. Why didn't I see it before? *That's* the appointment you keep talking about. Which is why you don't want me to come."

At that moment he decided, stubbornly, against his will: I'll bring her along. But he knew he wouldn't do it.

"I'm not married," he said.

With her face now eggshell white, and the tip of her nose red, her allure was washed away, as if a photographer had caught her grimacing.

"You're meeting your wife."

"Right. For a one-night stand," Tom snapped. "Then back to you."

But Happy didn't change her tune. She just decided to use off-beat lyrics.

"I'll call her the Over the Rainbow Girl. Because that's where she is in this muddled, magic world. Over the rainbow. She's in some happy-happy land because she can have you all the time all for herself. I know it."

He took a deep breath, blew it out slowly from puffed cheeks, showing his impatience with her.

"Pray tell, describe this process of intellection. How the cogs of your cogitation function, cognitively speaking."

"You're making fun of me," she sang. "Being sarcastic again."

"I'm not."

"You are. You're purposely using big words I don't under-stand to intimidate me. But that doesn't faze me because I have another power."

"Okay. Simply put. One: you're off base. Dead wrong. Two: what makes you come to this conclusion? Or as the great French epistemologist Henri-Jacques Ezra Shultish puts it in his classic *La Fille Yéménite*: How do you know what you think you know?"

"How do I know what I know? And I hope your French friend won't get epist off if I drop the think. And you're being sarcastic again. You can't resist it, can you? Because a guy like you is the marrying type. I can tell by your face. Just by looking at you. A guy like you, gals grab up. That's my line of reasoning."

"Sorry, but your line has sunk. I told you, I'm not married."

"You're not married?"

"No . . . I'm engaged." But he saw at once he shouldn't have said it. Again he saw the colors in her face changing.

"I'm pulling that shapely leg of yours. Joking."

"Really?"

"Really." He held up his hand. "Cross my heart! Not even engaged. Absolutely, wholly, entirely, Happy-ly single."

She kissed him.

"A kiss of truce or a kiss of peace?" he asked.

"Not a kiss of peace," she said. "Not truce either."

"Are you this way with every guy?" he wanted to know. "Or just with me?"

"You're the lucky one," she said. You'd think she'd fake a thinking pose before she replied. Bring a finger up to her lip like he did when pretending to think something through. But no, she thought squarely on her feet. In fact, chin up, hands at her sides, she said, "Each relationship creates its own vibes. I'm not the same. You make me different. You inspire me to do, to say, certain things. . . . Are you the same?" she challenged.

He didn't want to admit. "Hard to say."

"But no," she sang with a bite in her voice, "Mister Tommy won't strip his self-protecting armor, will he? Lest, God forbid, he bares his soul to someone."

"That's just what I mean," he shouted. "This sarcasm. Is it really you? Are you always this way?"

"No," she shouted back. "I told you. You inspire me. What're you worried about, what're you afraid of?" Arms on her hips now. "Someone—me!—getting to know the real you?"

"You know more about me than I do."

"Bullshit! My God! I don't even know what schools you went to before Dartmouth. Dartmouth, Dartmouth, that's all I hear is Dartmouth, Dartmouth, Dartmouth."

"I'll bring you my report cards.... You know what, I'm sick of your sarcasm."

Back to eggshell white, her face. His nastiness surprised her, maybe even frightened her.

"*My* sarcasm. God, what about yours? Your sarcasm is so sarcastic, if it was bottled . . . it . . . it . . . it would break the bottle."

He licked his lips, said nothing to rebut.

"We're fighting again," she tried to say lightly. "It's our second or third."

"But not. . . ."

"Our last, is what you were going to say."

Tom stamped his foot, but he was barefoot, so it made no impression, except on his heel, which now hurt. He slammed his fist down on the mattress.

"See what I mean? See what I mean about gratuitous argumentativeness, looking for a fight, putting nasty thoughts into my words where none were intended? Understand?"

"I would if I knew what 'gratuitous' meant."

"Absolutely unwarranted. Now why in hell did you assume I was going to say, 'But not the last'?"

"Because that's how the tone of the conversation was going. Sarcasm for sarcasm. . . . Okay. . . ." She relaxed now, wanted to make amends. "Sorry. What were you going to say? Honest now."

"Here we go again. . . . Why 'honest now'? Do you expect something less than honesty? Say it!"

She didn't say.

"I thought it was honesty that marked our relationship. . . ." He dropped his voice. "I was going to say: But not any others."

She looked at him with a tell-it-to-the-Marines expression. Pressed her lips, stuck out those kissable pink lips unmarred now by crimson streaks, head tilted, one eye slightly closed. He didn't have time to see any arch in her eyebrows that would have completed that look of incredulity. But she didn't say a word. Perhaps the fight had gone out of her. Perhaps she just wanted him to hold her close.

Then she said, sadly:

"When I fight with you, all my magic goes out of me. I lose everything. Remember I told you about how every person has a song in his heart. I want that song in my heart to be sung. I want to release that song in my heart. So don't break my heart. Please. If you break my heart I die."

Later that night he took a walk around the Piazza. It was late. The moon was full. A roseate haze hung over it like a veil. It would be hot tomorrow. The sky blue velvet. Two orchestras on opposite sides of the Piazza competed for attention. One played jazz, led by a clarinet, with dozens of onlookers standing behind the tables, while only a handful of patrons sat. Waiters stood, hands on the back of empty white wrought iron chairs. On the Bell Tower side, Florian's orchestra played their usual Viennese schmaltz. They probably hadn't learned a new tune in years. Why was he here all alone, waiting for a phantom meeting to take place next evening, a rendezvous whose outlines were shaped more by imagination than reality? Around the Piazza he went, stopping to gaze at the reflections of the palace and the basilica in the rain puddle from the afternoon's quick downpour.

Early tomorrow morning, he imagined, in the magical quiet of a Venetian dawn, the sweepers with their odd long straw brooms,brooms made in fairy tales, would sweep away the puddles, the detritus and last night's shadows, preparing for the glorious Festa day and its enchanted night.

2. Tall Aunt Maria and the Amazing St. Bernard

He figured if he left early, said nothing, it would be assumed that everything was all right. See you later, he said casually, and went out straight to San Marco to look at the fountain where in a couple of hours, he'd meet Zoe.

The crowds in the Piazza were thick. Tourist from every country. Italians from the heel of the boot, thick-faced peasants with a slightly dazed look, Japanese with camcorders, Senegalese selling imitation Gucci bags. The old and young, the pretty, the hags. Here gelati sold, there souvenirs of Venice. Wandering peddlers hawked everything. What did wandering peddlers sell? What didn't they sell? Tiny chains with ten stamp-sized photos of Venice that folded out, accordion-like. T-shirts. Tiny gondolas. Tin repros of the Doge's Palace. Even seeds to feed the pigeons. Groups of young celebrants came by, five arm in arm, singing Italian ditties at the top of their lungs, stopping groups of other singers and challenging them to rhymes. At each singing contest people gathered to listen and, if they approved, applaud.

Everywhere on the Piazza little tables with bottles of wine. For one thousand lire you could have a glass and the money went to a local charity. Happiness was everywhere. In the swagger of the youngsters, the tunes in the gondolas, laughter in the lanes. It fluttered in the air like tiny aspen leaves, like pink dogwood blossoms in a rain. With ease one could pluck joy from the air. Tonight Zoe. Zoe tonight. Dusk in the Piazza. Less than two hours to go. He felt an arm slipping into his. Turned and saw Happy. So she had followed him. At first he thought he would explode with rage. Tear his arm away from her in anger and run. But he restrained himself. If he bolted, he knew, he would tear himself away from her forever. There was plenty of time between now and 10:30 to explain that he had to be by himself. Never mind, he'd see the fountain later.

Hand in hand, they floated. She had put on a smidge of lipstick, he saw. Masked and unmasked people greeted them. One fellow in a tricorn hat sank down on one knee and serenaded Happy. Then, either by his volition or Happy's, or by that of the ouija board that controlled both their movements, they walked across the square to one of the calles that led to the Grand Canal. Now they strolled along the water, moving slowly with the rush-hour thick crowds. Then, just as Happy had appeared from nowhere, he found that she was gone. How had he become separated from her? He must have turned to look at another group of singers and thought that Happy was with him because someone held on to his sleeve. He stood on the wall side of the canal. The lights were bright not only from the street lamps but also from torches that young Venetians bore aloft like trophies, and what seemed like hundreds and hundreds of gondolas, rowboats, motorboats, rafts, each alight with torches or kerosene lamps, turning night into day, filled the lagoon and the Grand Canal. By now the traditional chain of gondolas from Venice to the Redentore Church was already starting to form across the lagoon.

At night the ambience was eerie, a romantic, movie-like setting. Some people held torches, some wore masks. One man stood and stared at him, as if saying, Admire my mask. "That's a nice mask you have," Tom said. "That's not a mask," he replied. "That's my face." Next thing he knew he was separated from the people near him, as if a wave, indeed it was a human wave, had come between them. What happened next stunned him. His first thought was: here, in Venice? A powerful hand covered his mouth, another caught his shirt collar, twisted it and pushed him forward around the corner to a dark alcove. Though in a fog, he managed to lift both his hands and wave, like the Pope greeting a crowd. He felt himself pressed into a small triangular enclosure next to a wall —dumpster?—but he couldn't scream or say a word. In his dream-state, Tom fought back, shooting out, swinging. His antagonist didn't go for his wallet but punched him once in the solar plexus. He rode a parachute downspinning into a different world. Was it the wine he had sampled here and there at the endless bazaar, the city-wide block party that helped him reach this dizzy state? Or was it the hands around his neck slowly squeezing, squeezing his throat, he helpless to defend himself? But in the last spark of light the name of Zoe was illuminated.

Now that he was choking, it was time for the film of his life to pass before him. He knew why he had been brought here. It was his punishment. Zoe is here getting even with me, he thought, on the day she's supposed to meet me. For the first words he heard were not from his unknown attacker or from cries from within, but words that Zoe had given him, her only words of recrimination, he hearing Zoe saying not her own words, but Zoe quoting Tolstoy, no, not even Zoe quoting as she stood by the balustrade overlooking the dry ice-skating rink at Rockefeller Center twenty-four years ago just before they parted, but the book that reads itself, the book speaking its own title, *God Sees the Truth but Waits*, uttered in a deep Russian basso. And now the truth had come. That was her hint to him. That retribution would come. Here, by an unknown hand, was the hand of God working against him. This was the revenge, the punishment, for his deed, his misdeed, his abandonment of Zoe. Did he accept his fate? Not on your life. Or his. With his last strength, I must get to Zoe, as the fingers pressed tighter, squeezing the breath out of him, he kicked out at the groin of his assailant, then heard in the back of his mind, where memory remembers, words that sounded like "can" and "kin" and "doo," and then, as the life stuff in him just barely floated above the point of no return, he heard Happy's voice calling "Tom, Tom, Tom," and felt her hands under his armpits, urging him forward. He heard her calling his name and his name revolved in his head like a distant lasso circling above him, not really his name, maybe yes, floating far away, a name that did not belong to him anymore because the life in him was slowly being sucked away. But still he kept hearing Happy saying, "Come, come, come, quick, pull yourself together . . . up, up, up and out," until he felt himself being pulled forward by a strength beyond his own. Up he went, then down, and landed on the pavement. "Come quick," Happy urged him. Tom moved in a daze, saw everything through a silk curtain. The world spun slowly before him. His throat was raw; so raw he could barely swallow. Still, he sensed he was free.

They stumbled through the calle until they came to Campo San Stefano, where three roly-poly girls stood before the church.

The triplets approached.

"Is he ill?" one of them asked.

"Yes. Not well."

Happy spoke softly to the girls.

"It was she who saved me," Tom whispered in Italian.

"*Brava, brava, brava,*" the three girls said, one after another. "Come with us. Our aunt will help you."

Tom hesitated. Happy pulled forward but he stood still. Yes, there was celebration in the street, but who knows what kind of people he could meet? The masks people wore—stiff, threatening, expressionless—seemed to rub off on the others and they all looked eerie. Would it be a mistake to go? Maybe they worked for the same men who had attacked him. As if in response, one of the girls pulled out a three-sided mirror. He looked at himself, saw two profiles. He looked so drawn he figured he'd take the chance.

Tom nodded at the triplets. He took one step, felt the street bending up toward him, the cobblestones slowly butterflying toward his face and then descending. Happy took him by the arm and they followed the three girls to a tiny courtyard.

"Up to the third floor," one of the girls said.

"No elevator?"

"There are no elevators in private houses. Only in hotels."

Tom didn't remember climbing the stairs. Even walking straight on the pavement was like climbing stairs. Everything turned like a corkscrew. He felt he was being guided up a spiral staircase.

One of the triplets opened the door. In the hallway stood a tall, thin woman, six foot six, in high heels. "Nice to see you," she said. Her pale blue dress made her white skin seem whiter than the white shawl around her shoulders. Tom remembered her eyes were light blue, but could not tell if they were cool cerulean or kindly blue. Maria was her name, she said. She patted Happy on the hand and nodded to Tom.

The three girls quickly and in one voice told Maria what had happened. At once Maria said, "Of course, I'll help you. We don't let people die in Venice before their time."

Then Maria cupped the palm of her hand carefully under Tom's chin, picked him up and, moving forward quickly, stretched him out in the air like a billowing cape, like a sheet being thrown in the air over a bed, like a furrier draping a mink on a floor, a Turk unfurling a prayer rug—that's how cloth-like, light and floaty Tom had become in the woman's hands. In the air, he fluttered like a flag. As soon as he touched the sofa, floated down on it like a goosedown featherbed, Maria emitted a little two-toned screech and a huge white St. Bernard bounded into the room and headed for Tom.

Happy ran between them. "Please! Stop him! Can't you see

he's weak?"

Another double squeak by Maria and the dog stopped, as if turned to stone.

"Don't be afraid," said Maria. "It's a good dog, a beneficent animal. With medicinal capabilities, cures under his tongue. Can't you see he's all white, like a doctor in his smock?"

"Yes," said Happy, "but a butcher also wears a white smock."

"If you're suspicious, test him. Try."

"But I'm not sick. I feel fine."

"Wonderful. Then you'll feel even better. Bend down on your haunches."

The dog came up to Happy, sniffed her face and licked it with his long flat tongue.

At once Happy felt a high, rising above herself. "Mmm," she said, moaning sweetly. "I see what you mean."

"Ready?" Maria asked Tom.

He nodded. The St. Bernard bent down to Tom's shoes. With his teeth he took hold of the laces and, by shaking his head back and forth, loosened them, then gently removed Tom's shoes and peeled off his socks. He began huffing on the toes, from the big toe to the pinkie and, then back again as though playing an ocarina. Musical sounds like Papageno's fife in the *Magic Flute* came out of Tom's toes. Slowly, the color returned to his face. Gone the pallor, enter ruddiness. He put his hands under his head and propped his head up. Took a breath, insucked an endless space of fresh clean air from the pine forests of Arosa, from Bellagio on Lake Como, from mid-ocean, from the Grand Teton mountain peaks near Jackson Hole, from the high steppes of Uzbekistan, where nor man nor beast had trod, air so pure and pristine it cleared his head, focused his sight. He swallowed. His throat no longer hurt. He bounded up, shouted, "I feel fine!" But that wasn't enough. He jumped up and down three times and yodeled till the walls shook and he saw Alpine cows with great bells around their necks lumbering slowly down a pasture. Then he sang, "I feel terrific! Never felt better!"

Another thrice-uttered *"Brava"* from the triplets, hard to say if they said it together or one after the other, and tall Aunt Maria standing on tiptoe said with a smile from somewhere near the ceiling, "I am so pleased."

Happy stood on tiptoe too and shook the woman's hand. "Thank you, Maria. But just let me ask you one question. When the dog approached me, he licked my face; when he came up to Tom he went for his toes. Why?"

Maria laughed. So did the three girls, echoing, "*Perché, Perché, Perché.*" Even the St. Bernard came out and smiled.

"He's scent oriented," said the aunt. "The spot that smells most, he goes for. Your face has the perfume of lipstick so we went for your face. But because of what happened to your husband, he perspired, sweated, so the smell was concentrated in his feet and that's why the dog went for his toes."

"But what about the music? The flute-like sound when the dog blew on Tom's toes?"

"What about the music!?" Maria said in a sharper tone. "What about the dog? What about his tongue? What about the cure under his tongue? Can't mysteries be left resolved? Must every question be answered? Is everything subject to analysis? Shall I ask you the secret of how you—?" and her finger became pointy as a pencil and her nose as pointy as her finger.

The longer she pointed, the paler Happy became. And then Maria stopped before Happy became white as marble and still as stone.

And then they were out the door, down the steps, standing in the courtyard.

"What time is it," Tom asked.

"It's 9:49."

"Still 9:49? How's that possible?"

"Time stopped," she said.

"Let's go," he said. "I got that meeting at 10:30. My clothes are all sweaty. I've got to change. Let's move."

Three windows opened on the third floor and the triplets sang out into the quiescent night in a melody from Gilbert and Sullivan:

"Then take a gondola. Turn right and by the first bridge you'll see a gondolier."

"What time is it?" Tom shouted up to them.

"Twenty-one forty-nine," they sang back.

As they walked his thoughts gathered, rolling downhill like balls of snow, faster and faster, larger and larger. It was Zoe's revenge. He knew it, no doubt about it. She had planned it, thought it out, hired the goons, maybe even watched. She parades with the guy near the fountain, spots me, nods to the goon, who proceeds to follow me. Maybe just the thought of him being hurt and humiliated sufficed her. He recalled an old moral conundrum. If for a great reward, could someone kill another human being far away with just a push of a button? No blood, no screams, no seeing, no guilt. But of course there was a fourth dimension to this grid. Was the person at the other end terminally ill, waiting to die? Was it a murderer sentenced to death? Or was it an innocent person with clean hands on the other side of the world? Maybe that's how Zoe handled it. From far away. But then Tom shook his head. What's wrong with you? he reproached himself. He leaned over the bridge. Where's that gondolier they promised? Would Zoe go to the expense of a trans-Atlantic journey, with all the attendant energy and costs, just to hire some thugs to hurt him? On the very night they were to meet? The silver anniversary of their first magical meeting here in Venice?

He tried to stop his suspicious thoughts. "Maybe let's walk," he said to Happy, "let's not lose any more time." But Happy calmed him. They said there's a gondolier. Trust them. Those suspicious thoughts, he tried so hard to stop them but his anger at Zoe was just too sweet to stop. Being furious with her, oh how good it felt. So why should he cease and desist? Why did Zoe have to do that? What was the point of waiting twenty-five years for revenge? Good Lord, she could have done that during any one of the first years when the wound was still fresh. Why wait for when he was getting ready for a great reunion with her, a sign that all was well and forgiven? But go figure out a woman! Who knew what kind of crazy thoughts ran through their heads! What manic energy drove the engine of their feelings. The only thing predictable about them was their unpredictability.

But wait! Wasn't there another possibility? That not Zoe but the other woman in his life had orchestrated this? To make him miss his appointment, furious that he didn't want to take her out on Festa night? Who knows what she was capable of with her gypsy strength?

"Come on! Where's that gondola?" Tom complained.

"It'll come, don't you worry."

And then he remembered that it was she, Happy, who had

saved him. If not for her, who knows where he'd be now. He put his arm around her. "My Lord! I didn't even thank you for saving me. How'd you do it? Can you tell me?"

"Sure. I'm not like Aunt Maria. I share the mystery. Simple. I made myself invisible, like I told you last week, floated into that enclosure, and began gouging his eyes until he let you go. And I gave him a knee in the balls too. The guy didn't know what hit him. And then I pulled you out. . . . Boy, are you heavy. . . . It was good you raised your hands when he dragged you off. That way I was able to see you."

"Invisible? Did I really hear you say invisible?"

"Yeah."

Invisible, my foot! But after hearing his toes play flute-like notes he was willing to give her the benefit of the doubt.

3. Guess Who's the Gondolier?

It began to rain. The rain splashed and bounced on the narrow dimly lit canal like gems seeking exit from the water. Then, from the darkness, he appeared. A gondolier in a red-banded straw hat scudded toward them, seemingly unaware that Tom and Happy were there. He stopped rowing and looked up.

"Gondola? Good price for Festa." And then the gondolier, his straw hat pulled down low over his face, opened up a bright yellow umbrella.

He had an elegant craft, Tom saw, a shiny black gondola with purple cushions front and back, silver-rimmed seats, and a crimson Bokhara carpet on which he stood.

Tom and Happy walked down the three stone steps into the gondola. The gondolier gave Tom the yellow umbrella. Where had he seen it before?

"Can you rush? I'm in a hurry. To the first small canal left of the Piazza."

"Sure. It'll take me no time. . . . Umm, miss, you can't sit in the back."

"Why?"

"Back is wet. Sit here up front with me."

"But it's wet in the front too. That's not logical."

"Logic-shmogic. I'm not a philosopher, I'm a comedian. And, anyway," he looked up, spreading his hands. "It's stopped raining."

"That yellow umbrella looks so familiar. . . . Where'd you get it?"

"The Rockefeller Center rink café. . . . I used to be a singing waiter there."

Tom bent forward, looked under the low-slung hat and saw who the gondolier was.

"My God! I *thought* I recognized your voice. You're Jack Benny! I thought you were dead."

"I am. I lost a thousand lire on my last fare and it killed me."

"How come you're gonding a gondola if you're such a famous star?"

"Our show is off during the summer and an extra buck never

hurts." Benny pushed off from the walls of the embankment and began rowing. "I tried driving a taxi here and got nowhere. . . . Just a joke, kids. It's not even mine, it's my writers'."

"Are you still thirty-nine?"

"Of course."

"Even when you're dead?"

"Especially! You don't get any older when you're dead.... How old are you, son?"

"I'm thirty-nine too."

"And you're alive?"

"Sure. At least I think so."

"Can you prove it?"

"Well, I'm talking to you, am I not?"

"That's no proof. I'm talking to you too. And am I alive?"

"Wait a minute," Happy said. "Now *that's* logical. I thought you were not a philosopher?"

"I'm not. But comedy doesn't exclude occasional logic. How did Seneca put it the other day? 'Nothing human is foreign to me.' But seriously folks, don't take me too seriously. What I meant was, can you prove you're thirty-nine, son?"

"Sure. Twenty-five years ago I was fourteen," said Tom.

Jack Benny stopped rowing. He thought for a while, then said, "Hmm! I'll buy that. . . . I can live with that. . . ." And he began imitating his valet Rochester's gravelly voice. "Boss, how old are you? 'Thirty-nine.' 'Thirty-nine?!'" Benny beautifully mimicked Rochester's classic screech of surprise. "Can you prove it, boss?" 'Sure I can prove it. Twenty-five years ago I was fourteen and I remember it was exactly one year after my Bar Mitzva.' 'Ha, ha, ha, that's rich, boss.'" Jack Benny began rowing again. "Hmm, I like that. My writers will *love* it."

"That Bar Mitzva addition," Tom said, "was very good. That made it funnier."

"Thanks. That's the difference between a philosopher and a comedian. A comedian is funny *all* the time. . . . So where is it you'd like to go, folks?"

"Take us to Rochester."

"He's working now. Driving a taxi. I gave him my old Maxwell."

"Driving a Maxwell in Venice?"

"Yup. He's got no competition. He's the only taxi driver in town."

"But he can't go anywhere. You know you can't drive in Venice."

It was as if Jack Benny were waiting for that line. He began laughing. "You can't drive my old Maxwell either."

"We meant the Hotel Rochester, not your valet. On that little canal I mentioned before."

"Oh, all right. A man can't even joke any more. . . ."

"Can't you hurry, please?"

"What's the rush? On Festa night no one rushes."

"I've got an appointment at 10:30."

"With whom?" asked Jack Benny.

Happy leaped forward.

"With my partner. I've got to deliver an important message."

Jack Benny rowed with long sure strokes. He rounded a corner with the traditional cry of "Oi-ee" and smiled proudly at Tom and Happy.

Tom thought of what to say to Jack Benny. He loved him as a kid, watched every one of his TV shows, and here he was rowing him in a gondola and he had nothing to say.

"I loved your film, _Come Blow Your Horn_. Caught it on the You're Never Too Late Show."

"You did? Well, it wasn't very successful. . . . That makes it three people who saw it."

"Who's that?"

"You, me and Rochester."

"Make it four. I saw it twice."

"Twice!? I can't beat that. Even I wouldn't see it a second time. I couldn't even pay Rochester to see it twice."

"How much did you offer him?"

"Never mind!"

"I also loved you in your cameo appearance in _Around the World in Eighty Days_."

"Well . . .," Jack said in his signature melody. "I'm already tempted to let you ride for free . . . but! But I'm not Oscar Wilde and I _can_ resist temptation. . . . So ... you saw _Come Blow Your Horn_. . . . Isn't that something? . . . Did you watch it alone?"

"Of course. I didn't want to lose a friend."

Jack Benny laughed. "Hmm. . . . I like that line too . . . and I'm glad I thought of it."

Tom ran his fingers over the purple cushion. No wonder he chose this gondola. When he first met Zoe, he told her about a love story he'd read that was set in Venice. It wasn't so much the plot or the characters that stuck in his mind—he even forgot the name of the story and its author—but the description of the comfortable gondola with its purple velvet cushions. He never forgot those sunset purple cushions and the slate green waters of the Grand Canal framing the gondolier.

"I love your cushions," Tom told Benny. "This purple color is stunning."

"I got it from a writer fellow named Sholom Aleichem, you know the guy who wrote 'Tevye in Venice.' Mr. Sholom Aleichem took these cushions right out of his story and gave them to me. . . . Here we are, the Hotel Rochester. And, please, no bargaining on the fare. Dying twice won't be good for my ratings. . . ."

Tom stood, about to step out of the gondola.

"What time is it?"

Jack Benny pulled out his pocket watch. "Exactly 9:49. I told you it'll take me no time."

"And how much do we owe you?"

"That'll be a thousand dollars, please."

"What?" Tom shrieked. "I don't even have a thousand dollars to my name."

"Oh, all right. Then make it a thousand lire. Who needs money when you're dead?" And then Jack Benny added, "By the way, have you seen Napoleon tonight?"

"No. Is he in town too?"

"Tom Sawyer? P.T. Barnum? Hemingway? Nachman of Bratslav? Hester Prynne? There's lots of us making the rounds tonight. We've all got the same agent. . . . Oh, never mind the money. You're the first person to recognize me here. And you saw my picture."

"Twice!"

"No one knows Jack Benny in Venice," Benny said sadly.

"Maybe it's the masks," Happy offered.

"The ones we're wearing, or the ones people wear?"

Tom looked at Happy. He was at a loss for an answer. If the

deceived wore masks as well as the deceivers, who was fooling whom?

"Isn't it hard for a man of your age, you've been thirty-nine for forty years, to gond a gondola?"

"Well, at least the canals are easy going. Last week I was up the creek. We did our show on the River Styx with Charon as our special guest and boy was that rough sailing. . . ! Well, good night, folks, we're running a little late, so we'll see you next Sunday at seven."

4. The Pigeon As Messenger

Step out on the street, into the smallest calle, and feel the excitement of people moving, singing, laughing. Soon Zoe. Even the night before was one of plosive merriment, as if proximity to the actual festive day were infectious and like a fuse spreading its spark, it affected the hours before the great day. And now, tonight, clerks and shopkeepers, bellboys and chambermaids, people on the street were on a kind of high, since good mood was contagious and all conspired to make this good cheer catching. Soon Zoe. Only illness was contagious, he had observed. Not good health. There had never been a pandemic of salutary health, but here in Venice, on the Festa del Redentore in mid-July, with people challenging one another with chanted verses and laughing at the antiphonal responses by the quays and in the square, on the narrow canal-side paths, on bridges, in the calles, from people gliding in gondolas to those on the walks, Tom saw the closest thing to the wildfire spread of good feeling, good cheer and good health that he had ever seen. Any minute now, the sun. A conspiracy of non-silence, an electric humming, a rumor in flight, people passing the word, word of mouth winging: there's good feeling in Venezia, joy in the city, thick in the air. Zoe, Zoe, laughter and gaiety in such abundance it could have been cut into tiny ribbons or put in balloons and sent sailing over the palazzos and canals, up to the golden statues that hovered above—and guarded—La Serenissima, the Queen of the Adriatic.

I'll kiss her, hug her, walk with her. We'll go to our café and have her favorite gelato and then, at 12:30, just like we did last time, at the Scuola San Stefano, we'll hear the traditional Festa night Bach Partita and the Vivaldi concertos that pulled our hearts together and made them one.

It was 10:30, 35, 40. Time may stand still for us, he thought, but for Zoe it doesn't. Where could she be? He turned, looked for both Zoe and Happy. After he had changed his clothes, Happy had gone out the door with him, then the sly little witch said she'd changed her mind. She'd let him go by himself. But he didn't trust her. She could not reign in her curiosity, nor her suspicious jealousy. Happy would show up again.

He watched the pigeons, tried to lose himself in the pigeons. What would Venice be without pigeons? They were another constant in Venice, like the arched windows, the palazzos and the canals. Tom singled out one pigeon, tried to follow it. This one would become his friend. Maybe it was the one he'd seen years back with Zoe, and it had flown the ocean to tell him the news. Maybe it would report if Zoe showed up. If it rose now and flew above its fellow pigeons and landed at the foot of the fountain—that would signal Zoe's coming. He kept his eye on the pigeon. It poked its head forward, now pecking at grains thrown its way, aggressively moving so that its fellow birds scattered. Go, rise, fly, Tom urged. Tell me Zoe is on her way. But then came another swirl of birds. Some pigeons walked away, others scattered like billiard balls and he lost his bird, the one that would signal Zoe's coming.

Wait a minute! Where's the fountain? On his first day in Venice first thing he did was go straight to the Piazza to look at the fountain where two weeks hence he'd see Zoe. To fix it in his mind, lest God forbid he'd forget where it was. But now the fountain wasn't here. What in heaven's name had they done with that famous landmark? How can you remove *the* fountain from Italy's most famous square? He looked again, but the place where he imagined the fountain to be was empty—he saw only the large rectangular paving stones of the Piazza. And how was it possible that Zoe, only a year after being there, agreed to meet him at the fountain? Had she forgotten the city so quickly? Had she accepted that as a landmark, knowing that there was no fountain in the Piazza, purposely agreeing so as not to refuse him to his face? In other words, a ruse?

No fountain. No fountain, no Zoe. A wave of panic sheared him, sour in the back of his throat. How could he have made such a stupid mistake? He could have sworn there was a fountain at the front center of the square, in a line with the Bell Tower and Florian's Café. Or could her forgetting and his forgetting stem from one wavelength because they were really one?

But wait. There were some work zones fenced in by orange netting scattered on the Piazza, like the Con Ed canvas-covered work fences in New York. Perhaps they had moved the fountain. The thought made him laugh. That was Zoe's self-mocking phrase when she got lost, couldn't find an easily numbered shop or site.

"They moved the grocery." "They moved the lateria." They moved the fountain, he heard Zoe saying. It was only when he walked to the northern edge of the square, to the left of the Basilica, that he saw a fountain. Zoe was right. They *had* moved the fountain. And put it further back, next to the church. Had it been removed for repairs, or was there a mystery going on in Venice, no less a mystery than the beauty of the place or of printed words conveying magic?

But in any case, there it was, and pigeons were dipping their beaks into the water, old people sat on the round bench rim of the fountain, and children were enjoying the spray.

10:45 now; 11 p.m. Where was Zoe?

Did she forget? he wondered. Perhaps she thought. . . .

You thought it was the *20ᵗʰ* anniversary, he said.

Yes.

And you came five years ago.

Yes.

But I wasn't there.

I know.

Were you disappointed?

What do you think?

You also didn't get your airfare reimbursed.

She laughed. That's right. . . . From the eighteenth year I was already counting the months, mentally tearing pages off a calendar.

I had a hunch that that is why you weren't there, he said.

And I waited for hours, walked around that fountain, Zoe said, practically wading through the pigeons. When they're on the ground, they're okay, but when they start fluttering and flying near your face, you wish they'd all turn into pigeon pie. And then when I got home I tried to figure out what went wrong. I just couldn't imagine you wouldn't be there, then I remembered maybe it was supposed to be the twenty-fifth anniversary of the child's birth.

He thought: She said "the child," not "our child." It was considerate of her not to rub it in. Even a pronoun like "our" could have a rough edge, despite the smooth, round sound of the word.

No, I specifically said twenty-five years after we first met in Venice, in 1967.

And then I thought it would be next year, twenty-five years after we met in Rockefeller Center.

But that's the same as choice A, and anyway that would put another year's wait to the plan.

She shrugged.

But maybe she couldn't come. Had family responsibilities. No money. No vacation time. Didn't feel up to it. Thought it a great idea, once, long ago, with him there, but upon further reflection considered it stupid. Why should she put herself out, and twenty-five years later too, for a guy who had abandoned her? And didn't ever want to know about the baby. What was the point of that three-thousand-mile plus rendezvous? To satisfy some romantic whim? Someone, somewhere, maybe in a book, maybe a movie, maybe even in real life had actually done this, actually carried out such a ridiculous adventure, and she was being subjected to it because of him. Again, he'd railroaded her, but this time she wasn't going along. Or maybe it was her husband. Yes, that was it. *He* wouldn't let her go,

And wasn't it possible, he thought, looking around, sifting faces, that they had just simply missed each other. Many people used the fountain as a meeting place. He didn't carry a sign like hotel chauffeurs at airports or railway stations. Suppose she'd looked for him but didn't recognize him after a quarter of a century. To be precise, twenty-four years since they'd last met at Rockefeller Center. He hasn't changed that much, runs through his head. Perhaps gained a bit of weight, but hair still dark brown and thick and wavy, the walk brisk and upright. And perhaps she's arrived early —why not?—and seen him on the Piazza with Happy. Perhaps seeing a man whom she faintly thought might be Tom but with a young woman attached made her assume it couldn't possibly be he. Or if she thought it was he, she decided to back off and not show up. No, he would not come to this special rendezvous, arranged so long ago, and have a young woman with him, adding a bit of salt to the wound, breaking that silent one-on-one concordat that they had entered into, compromising the privacy that two offered and three violated. Why did Happy attach herself to him like a leech? And maliciously so. What a nasty, stupid thing to do!

That was it, he decided. She'd seen him a day or so ago with Happy on the Piazza, realized it was Tommy with another woman, hung around a bit, and left. Disappointed she'd been; maybe even shattered. Because she'd never gotten married, hoped he hadn't either and was waiting, longed for that magic moment, like out of a novel or a myth, when after twenty-five years they would reunite *in the very same place they had met*, and a spark dormant all these years would ignite, call it spontaneous combustion, and music in the background from one of the café orchestras would accompany their embrace and long overdue kiss, as tears roll down the cheeks of all the sensitive women watching the screen.

He walked around the fountain—it was 11:15 p.m. now—not leaving it unattended for a moment. They had promised to wait for ninety minutes, one hour and a half. That was the *de rigueur* wait for a twenty-four-year appointment.

Now let's see if she'll show up, he thought. There were so many possibilities. Was she thinking of their date over the years, as he had? Did she to humor him say yea that day in New York and then add a sarcastic, Sure I'll be there, meaning: I'll be there for him like he was there for me. Or did she really want to go through with it but fell ill at the last minute? Or made the reservation then backed down a few days ago, realizing how crazy this idea was? With friends she couldn't have possibly discussed it, unless she told them that she'd made an agreement with an old college girl friend to meet in Venice in twenty-five years less one and had this wild urge to keep her promise.

The surprise he'd promised her years ago in New York had already been arranged. He hadn't quite formulated it in his mind when he uttered it in the Rockefeller Center ice skating rink when the ice season was months away and the rink was now dotted with rows of bright yellow umbrellas and a smooth parquet floor and café dining was taking place where the ice skaters would skate six months from now. But the idea had floated in the back of his head like an out-of-focus picture. Well, maybe it *had* been formulated. Out-of-focus is after all just a prelude to in-focus, a mere turn of the knob. In any case, it's the same picture. The surprise was this: he'd take her to the Danieli for dinner and maybe into that room they'd seen soon after they met. The bellhop had told them to take their time, excused himself, and departed. Tom took one look at Zoe, one at the inviting bed, and threw her down on it and kissed her hard.

"Some day," he said, "we'll spend a night here," he promised her.

Zoe got up, straightened the bed cover as if she worked there, ever the good girl, the upper lower class girl, not wanting to leave a tell-tale sign, not wishing to abuse her host's hospitality. She was red in the face, as if caught by the bellhop or the clerk.

"You're crazy," she said admiringly.

Would she spend a night with him? Probably not, but it wouldn't hurt to plan ahead. He could always cancel at the last minute. Then he realized with a start that he could neither stop the clock nor turn it back. You jerk, he scolded himself. Always off in dreamland. If she came at all, she would probably come with her husband, for what excuse could she possibly give for going off by herself? You see, the guy who knocked me up and made me have my baby alone, I met him a year later at Rockefeller Center after he came back from a year in London and we agreed on this kooky plan to meet in Venice in twenty-five years. That is, twenty-five years from the year we first met. My God, he thought, I hope she understood I meant Venice, Italy and not Venice, California. Of course, St. Mark's Square, she said and the Festa del Redentore. But he made the reservation for dinner and a one-night stay in any case. In fact, he did this the day he arrived in Venice, the very first thing he did after inspecting the site of the fountain in the Piazza. That is, after laying eyes on Happy sailing away on the vaporetto forever, vanishing from his life, he thought, but not his dreams. How he picked her out of the crowd crowding the railing, how he zeroed in on her, like tv cameras zero in on a group photo and pick out an individual with a coin of light, darkening at the same time everyone else, that's how Tom zeroed in on Happy on the vaporetto, even though he hadn't yet known her name.

The two bellstrikers atop the Piazza struck the half hour again. Why can't time stop now? he wondered. Please, please stop the clock again.

How would she look after twenty-four years? Probably pretty. He couldn't imagine her any less than pretty, certainly not middle-aged and blowsy, no. He would recognize her right away, and she him. But what if she came with her husband? That would kill everything, knock the Danieli caper right out of the window, through the Venetian blinds, to coin a phrase. Zoe would only have a few more lines around the eyes, the only sign of the passing of two dozen years. And her coming would signal her forgiveness. No, she couldn't, wouldn't possibly come with a husband, for she wasn't likely to have admitted having had a child out of wedlock. Or maybe she passed him off as a child from a husband who had died, perhaps killed in a war or in a plane crash. For how else could she explain going to meet a man? Unless she planned a vacation around the Festa del Redentore and just happened to bump into him by the fountain. How awkward that would be.

Hi.

Hi, there, Wow, this is amazing! How *are* you? Bill, this is my husband, Bill. I want you to meet, oh dear God, I know you, but I've forgotten your name.

Tommy. Thomas Manning.

Tom. Of course. How could I have forgotten? Bill, this is an old friend from college. . . . What are you doing here?

Waiting for you, Tom says.

Her jaw drops. Then he laughs. And she laughs, the crimson in her face subsiding now. And this laughter makes hubby Bill laugh. She sees he intended it as a joke but it wasn't a joke. When he makes a twenty-four-year date, he doesn't exactly expect the date to bring a friend.

11:45, 11:50.

How many different reasons can there be for a person not to show up? Let us count the ways. First off, no denying the inexorable, is death. Dead is dead. And no amount of will power can make the dead take a plane trip. Not even supersaver discounts or frequent flier miles. Even to Venice, of which it is said: See Venice and die! But if one dies first it's no go. Okay, enough of that. Let's not belabor the point. Second: illness, also a viable excuse. But down the list there could also be: forgetting (although how could anyone forget such an unusual appointment?), missed connections, an injury, a rail strike, a recalcitrant husband, a boss who cancels your vacation because of an emergency, a parent ill, a child needs tending, a sprained ankle just as you're leaving your hotel. Or, you want to go, you've been thinking of going for the last twenty-four years, but at the last minute you get, as the Russians say, chilly legs. God, there can be hundreds of reasons (noxious reasons, he says to himself, masked as excuses) for someone not being in a certain place at a certain time when she promised to be there. Look at any spot in Venice. Take the fountain on the Piazza or see an empty space under the arcade, and imagine dozens of reasons why that spot is empty now, whereas hours ago a young couple was hugging there.

And then, if the person doesn't show up at the appointed hour, how long do you wait? Ninety minutes, they'd agreed. God, the protocol of waiting in this case is so unusual. How do you handle a twenty-four year arc? How long do you wait? A week? A month? On the other hand, one would think that after a twenty-four-year wait one would be meticulous and even show up early so as not to take a chance and miss the guy who's been waiting a quarter century to see you again. Yes, that seemed reasonable, even desirable. In this case, you have to make up protocol as you go along. There are no set rules. Still, for such an unusual appointment you don't dare show up late. You come early. And if you're not there an hour later, you're not going to show up. But on the other hand, there were mitigating circumstances, see *supra*. Or suppose the vaporetto got stuck. A sudden fog. It's been known to happen, and then the vaporettos just stop going. And she comes running two hours later and you're not there. One must take that into consideration. There were so many pulls, pushes, possibilities, one should really sit with one's butt glued to the fountain and come up with a hundred excuses not to budge lest she show up late and not have to berate himself with the remark, If only I'd waited just a little bit longer I wouldn't have missed her.

Suddenly, he felt hands over his eyes. His heart surged. Oh God, a joy he had never known flowed through him. Through his closed eyes he kisses those lovely girlish hands. His eyes are wet. It was tears, he knew, but tears of bliss, happiness, ecstasy. He kept his eyes closed, turned, put his arms around Zoe and kissed her. He would walk around the fountain with her seven times and at the seventh he would slip the little ring he had prepared on her finger.

"I'm so glad you came," he said.

He opened his eyes.

A merry twinkle, that of a naughty girl, in Happy's eyes.

"How'd you know I was here?" He tried to control his voice.

"Where else do people meet?"

"Dozens of places."

"This is the best. . . ." Then, "I guess she hasn't shown up."

"He's late, I guess," said Tom. "It's good you came. You can do us a favor."

"Who's the us? You and her?"

"Stop it! You and me. There's a post-midnight, actually a 12:30 Bach and Vivaldi concert at the Scuola San Stefano. Where we were before. It's only about eight minutes from here, across four bridges, you'll see it on the right side of that rather large Campo San Stefano. Would you run over and get us two tickets? You'll see a big sign outside for the Bach Partita and other works. If my appointment doesn't show up during the next few minutes, I won't wait any more. I'll see you in front of the Scuola in about fifteen or so minutes."

Happy put out her hand for the money.

He didn't realize how nasty were the flies this evening. He hadn't noticed them here before. He swooshed one away that seemed to be blowing in his ear. Another landed like a dust mote in his eye. As he circled the fountain looking for Zoe, he was plagued, dammit, by little demons that tickled and annoyed him.

The fourth time around he saw Happy standing about twenty feet away, making her way through the crowd, approaching, holding up two tickets. She flew there and back, the witch. What now? She was frustrating his every move. Then a huge crowd of Japanese tourists came between them, with the leader holding up a bright yellow umbrella. Again Jack Benny? Tom wondered. They seemed to march on and on and Happy was momentarily lost in the crowd. What if he spots Zoe now? It would be uncomfortable for all three of them. For he was sure Zoe would be there alone. So sure was he, he never entertained the thought that maybe, maybe she would be with someone.

As he completes the slow totemic reprise of the seven times he had once walked around the fountain with Zoe, now at the seventh slow time around, looking here and there, the seventh time around, when the bride seals her bargain with the groom in Jewish weddings and, like adhesive tape, there was no undoing it now, the seventh time around he saw her, a circle of pigeons around her like the middle letter of her name, looking about expectantly, as if worrying that her date, who had just called the night before, might either be late or not show up. He greeted her, but not enthusiastically, not a Hollywood restaurant bear-hug hello where while hugging your friend your eyes roam the room to see who else you know, and not a New York restaurant genuine kiss-on-the-cheek greeting where during the kiss your eyes circumnavigate to see who's gotten a better table than you. Actually, he muted his enthusiasm. He wanted to hug her, just as he had wanted to years ago when he met her at Rockefeller Center and restrained himself. He knew it wasn't normal not to embrace. Why, one would even hug one's ex-wife when meeting her at a celebration. But if she displayed no sign of affection, neither would he. Still, though he wanted to hug her, he only shook her hand, looking tentatively into her eyes, wondering if it was really she. As he shook her hand, then put both of his hands on one of hers, to mitigate the formality somewhat, he said, So you remembered, but she said it first and he said, That's just what I was about to say. Both their voices sounded hyper as if twenty-four years of thinking and wondering were compressed into a few banal words and now they were stunned by the event that both had created. Then Happy materialized beside him and he saw Zoe looking at Happy with that bemused wonder in her eyes, as if asking him: Who is this? Your girlfriend or your daughter? He realized he'd been remiss in introducing them. How do I introduce them? he asked himself. Very carefully, he answered. Said: This is Happy. Happy, meet—just then a child ran into the flock of pecking pigeons that formed a halo around Zoe's feet, poking at the ground, and scared them away. The flutter of wings, the clutter of their flight, drowned out Zoe's name. Zoe had stepped back, hands up, protecting her face from the pigeons, when a souvenir vendor stepped between Zoe and Tom, followed by a flock of teenagers singing Festa del Redentore ditties. Like in a film when a man disembarks from a little boat and a wind comes and takes the boat farther and farther away from shore, so the distance between Tom and Zoe seemed to enlarge and the space between them filled with Venetians and tourists and photographers. By the time Tom thought of pulling from his pocket the rope with the lifesaver ring and throwing it to her, Zoe had disappeared.

He remembered his father had once taught him a moral lesson. Once, after the organic winter wheat he had planted had failed, his father counseled, "We'll try again." So he took the surprised Happy by the arm and walked around the fountain one more time, trying again, and met Zoe, who had returned. This time he minded his manners first and introduced Happy. "This is Happy," he said, remaining vague about who she was and how they were related. "And Happy, I'd like you to meet . . . " but now, once again, as he was about to utter Zoe's name, to sound out the vibrations of the first letter, one of the fluttering pigeons flying above them, just fed by a sympathetic tourist, flew toward Tom, plucked Zoe's name from the air as if it were a bread crumb, and to the tune of the twelfth stroke of the bell by Venice's ancient rooftop timekeepers, flew away.

But isn't a person's name his being? And with the flight of Zoe's name, so the flight of the selfsame. Before he could reach out to touch her, she was gone again.

A moment later, or perhaps at the very stroke of the twelfth gong, as the iron tongue of midnight tolled its bells, an explosion of light fell over Venice.

The fireworks from the San Giorgio church had begun, lighting up the sky with a shower of light.

He wondered if all the people going this way and that had some purpose to their peregrinations, or were they like senseless molecules moving helter-skelter just to get away from where they were to where they were not? Tom and Happy threaded their way through the crowds on the Piazza to the back calles. Here and there sparkles were thrown up in the air, lighting up the faces even more than the torches. They crossed four bridges and walked to the Campo San Stefano. Just then the Danieli popped into his mind. Would he see the inside tonight? And with whom? Something was happening to all his plans. He was supposed to take Zoe to the Scuola tonight and relive that concert of years ago. Where was she? Why had she shown up like a wraith and then slipped away from him? Or was his imagination on this magical Festa night so strong that storybook atmosphere was flooding his thoughts, blurring the line between hope and realization?

"Did you get good seats?" he asked Happy. "Let's see the tickets."

"No. You think I can fly back and forth?"

"You supposedly fly when you're invisible, or isn't that logical?"

"I save invisibility for lifesaving occasions, not ticket buying."

"Then what did you hold up?"

"A bank." She laughed. "My vaporetto tickets."

"To fool me. . . . But you said you'd go."

"I did not say I'd go. You told me to go. There's a difference."

"Why didn't you go? Why did you fool me?"

"I didn't like the idea of you wanting to get rid of me for half an hour."

"You're getting on my nerves."

"Only because you feel guilty about something. . . . Disappointed she didn't show?"

He toyed with the idea of smacking her. Now he knew why guys smacked their girl friends. With baiting like that the fist was the only answer. No verbal wit, no withering irony, no in-your-face sarcasm. Just the splendid epiphany of the articulated fist.

"Whoever didn't show up will show up in due time," he said.

She slipped her hand into his to show she didn't keep a grudge.

"What's a partita?" Happy asked cheerfully as they snaked quickly through the crowd of celebrants.

He told her to see a thesaurus. "You know what a thesaurus is?"

"Yes. A dinosaur. But how can I see one if they're extinct?"

He was so surprised he couldn't even laugh.

"A dinosaur?"

"Yes, you know, like a brown thesaurus?"

Delighted with her, he pulled her close. "I'll tell you what a partita is, but I'll do it like that former boss of yours did when he tried to show that guy who wanted to buy a left-handed cup his little mirror— ."

"The one that makes you upside down?"

"Yeah. Your boss answered that kook's question with—as you put it—an allergy. I too will answer by an allergy. . . . What's a señorita?"

"A little girl."

"Exactly. Señora, señorita. And a little Lola?"

"Lolita?"

"A little chick?"

"Chickeeta."

"Perfect. Now go by an allergy. If señorita is a little señora, a chiquita a little chick, a Lolita a little Lola, then a partita is a— ?"

"A little party."

"Bingo. Your prize is a kiss on the cheek. Right you are. You knew it all along. It's a little party. A musical party, given by Bach."

No sense giving her the other definitions, Tom thought. No need to reveal now the scores of meanings packed into that all-purpose word, including: a division, a parting, and a leave-taking too; not to mention a game, a match, and by pun extension, a fix-up, a set-up, an arranged marriage.

"Here we are. See how little time it took? You could have done it. . . . Now we'll have to stand on line and maybe not even get in."

Tom ran in to the Scuola.

"See?" Happy said, tailing him. "They're still selling tickets and the line isn't that long. No one's rushing to get seats to a post-midnight concert."

Two lines had formed for the two ticket sellers at two tables. Tom got on the right line. At one point he looked to the left and saw a woman staring at him whom he thought he recognized. When he saw her all his plans fizzled. Whoosh, they went like a smear of alcohol on a blackboard; they vanished at once. A surge, perhaps of fright in his heart, afraid to face her, if indeed it was she – otherwise, why should she be staring at him every few seconds? So Happy had done the right thing after all. Had she bought the tickets, he wouldn't be seeing Zoe now. And here was Happy again, pressing the 50,000 lire note into his hand. Wherever Zoe was, whenever he saw Zoe, there was Happy, interfering, breaking the spell. He took the money and watched Happy walk outside.

Zoe looks at Tom with a knowing, recognizing look, saying nothing. She isn't sure, but still there's a vibe of something in her face. He looks at—through—her. Why did you disappear before? He sees a little rill of apprehension run down her face. Her eyes narrowed, focusing more closely on him. She looked as if she were about to speak. *Excuse me, but are you . . .?*

He swallows. He felt he was at the cusp of something. A precipice, about to stumble. He realizes he can't go through with it. Why didn't you buy those tickets, Happy? They reached their respective clerks at the same time. He was perspiring; a steamy heat rose from under his shirt. Do you have tickets for Silvio Mosconi? he said loudly for her to hear, giving her a quick glance to see if she'd react with disappointment to the name. But apparently the woman had not heard. Her clerk gave her the tickets and she left the line. Only when his clerk asked, Could they be under any other name? did Tom excuse himself, mutter that he had not made reservations, and bought two tickets. He quickly ran out to the front of the Scuola to get Happy. On his way, he sensed that his soul was not at peace, perhaps because he remembered that feeling of un-ease that radiated out of the eyes of the woman who kept staring at him, that un-ease that pulsated rhythmically each time she raised her eyes and gazed at him. But it was not the same Zoe who had vanished half an hour earlier at the fountain, precisely at the stroke of midnight. This one was a different Zoe, but Zoe still, Zoe nevertheless.

The concert began with a cello concerto by Vivaldi. At once

the music overwhelmed him. If Happy could become invisible, so could he upon hearing Vivaldi. Each note clung to him like a discrete object until he was all music, devoid of materiality. Tom wondered where she was sitting.

But, like saving the chocolate topping for last, he did not look for her right away. First, he admired again the ceiling painted by Tiepolo and the twenty-foot panels on the walls, and only then did he slowly turn around. Now she was listening to the same sounds he was hearing, just like twenty-five years ago when they were last here in this hall. It was stupid not to have told her to meet him in front of the Scuola. It was an off-beat place, not crowded, no chance of them missing each other, which easily could have happened— perhaps did?—by the fountain, especially on the Festa del Redentore, when thousands of people crowded the Piazza. Last time they were here, they held hands, he not letting go of her small warm right hand, clasping it as if he wanted to hold it forever, they listening to a Vivaldi concerto which he hoped would never end. And now only the sounds united them, wherever she was sitting. But if she was here, why didn't she come up to him? She had been staring at him long enough on the line. Hadn't she recognized him? Had he changed that much? And why had he given a false name so loudly for her to hear as he leaned over the ticket table? Afraid, Thomas? All along you thought she would chicken out at the last minute, but that's exactly what you've done yourself. He looked to his left. Maybe she was again sitting next to him just like she had what seemed like yesterday at the evening concert. Wouldn't it be funny if Zoe were to his left while Happy was on his right, one big happy family unit, and he and Zoe made believe they didn't know each other, except during the music when the lights were down her hand crept into his and pressed it, or her foot moved slowly to the right until it covered his left shoe, while both stared straight ahead and even blinked with increased faux attentiveness, while he held Happy's hand and one electric current ran through all of them. He still could not understand why she hadn't acknowledged him at the line. Why did she stare at him, in pulses every twenty seconds, looking, then turning away, looking, then turning away, like a cat-and-mouse game people played on the subway? Why did she travel thousands of miles only to back out at the last minute? Or could it be he was still dizzy from his ordeal and

didn't really see her at the fountain or missed reacting to her
moue of surprise at seeing him at an adjoining line and not by the
fountain as planned, but noting his indifferent demeanor, turned
down the intensity of her stare, pretending she had made a mistake. It could also be, could it not?, that it wasn't Zoe at all on
line. She just hadn't shown up. Some objective observer could
perhaps explain it all away, but the bottom line was that Zoe was
not here. Maybe he would see her during intermission. His disappointment was Happy's joy. She was delighted that his "date"
(without quotes in her estimation; with, the view he wished to
project) had not come; she was quite open about her suspicions
that it was a woman and disaffected at this intrusion into their
privacy. But now he reached out and took Happy's left hand. It
was warm and soft. Its tanned skin was smooth, unblemished.
He felt like putting his lips to her skin and brushing his lips from
her wrist to her elbow. Her hand felt comfortable in his, as had
Zoe's.

He looked toward the orchestra, eyes on the solo cellist, a
thin man with a small, tight, intense face. His high cheekbones
gave his eyes an almost oriental cast; his prickly hair was sprinkled
with gray. The darkish, olive tone of his skin said: Sicily. His
manner of playing was even more intense. With lips compressed
and bow hand held out at an angle in the old fashioned way, the
one cellists used before Casals revolutionized bowing technique,
the cellist attacked the strings with ferocity, speed and skill. He
looked so familiar. Could it be that he was the soloist from years
back, when Tom had sat next to Zoe? He too had played with
closed eyes and manic drive, his head making short, snapping,
robot-like movements. Tom waited for him to rise and take a
bow. If he bent forward rapidly from the waist as if he were
unhinged and snapped back quickly, without a doubt it would be
the same fellow. When the applause began, the cellist stood and,
without smiling, just like years ago, snapped forward with a mask-
like stiffness to acknowledge the applause, then straightened up
at once. Yes, it was the same cellist. So time did not pass at all.
Everything was the same. Twenty-five years were bridged by that
unchanging cellist. Tom imagined greeting him and thanking him
for making time stand still. But perhaps the cellist would not like
that. He hadn't gone very far in the world, but had remained only

a small-time cellist in a small-town chamber group. And look how he had aged, become more wizened, his face tighter, while he, Tom, had remained the same. Time's erosion had skipped him by, while working its unmagic on the poor musician.

How he wished Zoe were sitting next to him so he could share this with her. You remember him, Zoe? He wondered if she would indeed remember the cellist with the hinged waist. But if Zoe couldn't remember if she had salted her buttered toast five minutes earlier, how would she remember a cellist whom she had seen but once?

Now the Bach Partita, arranged for chamber orchestra by Vivaldi, had begun. When Tommy first heard it with Zoe, the manuscript had just been discovered in a Venetian archive. The music cast a spell over him, a sweet floaty feeling, on the edge of sleep but not dozing, and he imagined Zoe's hand in his, why was Happy now sitting on his left when a moment ago she had been on his right, he had to look to make sure it was Happy's hand he was holding, but no, it was Zoe's, smiling at him now, pressing his hand with her old warmth, glad to be sitting next to him in this hall, glad to have been able to fulfill the dream articulated twenty-four years ago that they would meet in Venice on the night of the Festa, which he almost missed because he was trapped by some madman in a quirky kidnapping until rescued by Happy. She had saved him. He must not forget that. One must look at things from another person's point of view. How would he feel if the one evening that they had wanted to spend together Happy would say, Sorry, I have an engagement. Would he like that? No. He'd be jealous as hell. So there was a basis for her anger. Whither now, Tommy? he asked himself, thinking of Chaucer's Troilus saying: Which direction now, my life?

Like the hero of the Aschenbach (Eschenbach?) book, Tom didn't know if he was in a party in Venice or parting in Venice. Or was it just a partita, like the one by Bach that he had so looked forward to listening with Zoe? How many options a word could have, like a palace with seven times seven portals. Like one's life.

Zoe looked good, wore makeup. Her oval face sparkled, the blue eyes did it. But after a while, he saw the gray emerging, tiny microns of it invidiously seeping, leaching between the cells, not visible at once, but after an hour or so, the gray, the oldness, the tiredness of aging spreading over her face. She looked exhausted, not from overwork; it was her body that was tired. She looked drawn, either ill or recuperating. Then he realized why she looked old. Her very being was mourning. The pores of her skin mourned. She was mourning what could have been. What might have become of her had he not deserted her. Now it hit her, what he had done. Or was her face for him alone, like that eerie mirror Happy spoke of which turned your image upside down once the mirror was reversed as if it were a photo you were holding? No one else saw Zoe that way, except he, the author of her malaise. Why had she consented to this absurd and useless meeting, this expensive trip? Again he had directed and she had meekly followed. Once more, after twenty-five years, he had had his way again, in control, on top of every situation.

Funny how the Partita prompted memories. Not only prompted them but catapulted them forward, as if from a gigantic Roman war machine. The music turned the tap on and he could not shut it off. It was not like shutting eyes to stop seeing. It was more like trying to stop hearing sounds. Memories could not be turned off at will. No wonder they called it a flood of memories. Try shutting the faucet of a flood. And amid the flood, the book she'd given him when they parted at Rockefeller Center. Tolstoy's *God Sees The Truth But Waits*. Indeed, He does, but He waits a long, long time. Sitting next to Happy, he thought only of Zoe, so powerfully imagining Zoe at his side that all he had to do was turn to his left and she'd be there as she had been, in this same hall, even in the same row, twenty-five years ago when he was last with her here. He dared not look to his left. It was as if the god of perchance meetings had paralyzed his neck and he could not turn. For what would happen if indeed he did see Zoe sitting there next to him, smiling that little smile of pleasure and surprise? Then he forced himself to turn and—my prophetic soul!—there she was.

I was wondering how long it would take you to see me.

I was afraid.

Of what?

Seeing you. Of seeing you.

Still?

Yes. Still.

Don't. And she gave him a forgiving smile.

I can't help it. It still bothers me. I'm ashamed.

But you weren't when we met at Rockefeller Center.

It was too fresh then. I was young. It's grown in intensity over the years.

Is that why you gave that phony name at the box office table?

So she knew. He didn't have to answer. She knew his silence was affirmation.

You know everything, don't you?

Zoe didn't respond.

That's what so wonderful about us, he thought. We can talk without talking.

So why didn't you come up to me if you recognized me?

Because you initiated this entire scenario, remember? You told me to come. You didn't show up at the fountain and then you make believe you don't recognize me and give the ticket clerk a false name and at the top of your voice too, my God it was so obvious, to make me think I was mistaken about you. Well, I am mistaken about you. And always have been.

I can explain.

He seeks her hand in the semi-darkness as the Bach Partita scatters its notes like beneficent multi-colored flakes in the air but can't seem to find it. No matter how long his hands are he can't find her hand.

You see, I thought that you thought that since it was a festival I might be wearing a mask and that's why you didn't recognize me. And I thought you'd be wearing a mask and that's why I didn't recognize you.

What kind of idiotic logic is that? he reprimanded himself.

But Zoe put a finger to her mouth, signaling that she wasn't through.

And furthermore, I came three thousand miles to see Tommy Manning. I wasn't going to go to Silvio Mosconi and ask him if by some chance his alias was T. Manning. Or if he forgot his real name.

So you recognized me. After all these years?

Ch'io mi scordi di te? she said. Do you want me to forget you?

No iron can pierce the heart more than a phrase in its proper place, he thinks.

My God, you remembered, and tears misted his eyes and the musicians were blurred.

This thought brought on that, and that one led to Mozart. Why during a Bach piece thoughts of Mozart should flit through his brain he could not explain. Perhaps had he time to analyze the concatenation of thoughts he would have realized. Who could figure out the mind's percolations and meanderings? Perhaps because he had seen *The Magic Flute* in London before coming to Venice. Perhaps because like Tamino he too needed a guide. Who will be our guide and show the way? he thought as he became aware of the Partita again. Oh, the glory when the music continues. But when it stops, it dies. Like a girl at your side; as long as she's there —ecstasy. Once she leaves you, only ghosts dance. Like the Piazza. It's there when you're there. Once in the calles, the curtain is drawn.

The Magic Flute image, he recalls, it wasn't the first time it came to mind. It happened too while searching for Happy after she sailed away on the vaporetto his first day in Venice, disappearing as soon as he saw her. It must be an opera I'm in, he thought, one of the gloomy moments, the pit before the rescue, the dark before the lighting designer's superbright sunrise. Soon the gloom will vanish, he thinks, and I'll wake up to the joy I deserve. Oh, if only he had Papageno's magic bells and, upon playing that tinkly melody, he could convert the enemy camp to gaily dancing imps and beasts.

Why do we all smile when Papageno rings his magic bells? Because as we sit in the comfort of our seats in the opera house back in New York, wondering if we'll make it back safely to our parked car, and if the car will be there and, if it's there, if the windows will be intact and the locks unpicked, we secretly wish that we had a set of bells like that to neutralize the evil in this world, the muggers in this town, and with those magic bells giving out their sweet childish tune, we wish they could guide our own sweet destiny.

Which path in life does man choose—Papageno's "That's all I ask of life, a good drink, some food and a pretty girl, a turtledove beside me," or Panino's stagy, bookworld fairy tale "wisdom and virtue"? There must be a choice "c", Tom figured, that combines the best (or worst) of both.

The applause unmisted his eyes. He looked quickly at Happy, blissfully adoze. So Zoe didn't come, he concluded. Did I really think she would? he asked himself. Yes. Yes. Yes. But if what he had felt just now was real, she indeed had come, projected herself forward from wherever she was to be with him. And Happy once had said that astral projection was difficult! He looked at Happy again. If you can't re-embrace the past, he told himself, you have to fall back to the present.

He took Happy's hand and held it. A handful of wheat surpasses a dream banquet, went the Vermont farmers' saying. A real love is better than a phantom romance.

Toward the end of the concert, most heads were drooping. It was 1:45 am and people had had a long day. He felt he could have floated above the crowd and like Prince Charming kissed all the women and woken them up. Happy woke without his kiss. As the music flowed, he kept turning around, ostensibly to survey the audience's appreciation of Vivaldi and Bach, but actually checking out their appreciation of Happy. He was proud of other men's envious looks.

He also thought of the surprise on her face when he would lead her ("Where we going?" she'd ask. "Where?. . . Where? . . . Tell me. . . . Tell . . ." in her usual persistent, impatient fashion, never permitting him the joy of a surprise), lead her clear across the entire length of the Piazza San Marco, either under the arcade or through the open square, as if escorting her in a gavotte, a triumphal march, or a bridal procession, he hadn't yet decided which route he'd take, to the Danieli, where once again he'd replay with Happy a scene he'd played before with Zoe.

Just the other day, after she'd finished work and he met her in front of the Bell Tower, they walked along the Riva degli Schiavoni. She had walked by the Danieli on her own, she said, but never had the nerve to go in. His firm grip of her hand seemed to say, Just for that you're coming with me. Inside the lobby, he asked the clerk, without telling him he'd already made a reservation a couple of weeks ago for the night of the Festa, to summon a bellhop and show him a room. How history repeats itself. Like with Zoe, the room and the view floored her. "It knocked my socks off," was Happy's apt term. "It's gorgeous!" It must have been the same bellhop, for he too left them alone and as soon as he left the room Tom threw Happy on the bed. She bounced once, gave out a little scream of joy, and at once he was on top of her. She hugged him. "Do you think you could do a quickie before he comes back? I'm all wet for you." He just smiled and they both got up. She straightened the tapestried bedspread and smoothed it down.

After the concert they walked back to the now more subdued Piazza.

"Back to the fountain again? Still hoping?" she said, but he just pretended not to hear the dig and circled the fountain two times, maybe three, and headed for the Bell Tower.

6. Up in The Bell Tower, Again

At the Bell Tower, he stopped at the entrance.

"What now?" she asked.

"I want to take you up there now. It'll be a gorgeous view."

"But it's probably locked."

"Not on Festa night. . . . I'll go up to see if anyone's there. If I don't come down in five minutes, come up."

Up and up, spiraling upwards, his direction changing every minute, his way up inexplicable without the use of hands, spiraling he went, until he reached the top. Like twenty-five years ago, now too there was no one here. He looked in all directions, with Zoe's eyes. Felt her presence more than ever before.

A wave of regret, spiced with tears, washed over him.

"I'm sorry," he shouted into the night. "I'm sorry." Said it to the north, spoke it to the south. He sang it to the east and west, declared it to the city and the sea. He said it so loudly his words blocked his view, the letters of his words blindfolds on his eyes.

"I'm sorry, Zoe. Can you hear me saying I'm sorry? Please forgive me, Zoe."

She forgave him.

"Embrace me."

She did.

"Hold me tight."

She held him tight.

"Kiss me."

They kissed. A pure holy kiss, in the Tower, where church bells rang out all over Venice. Where prayers gathered and forgiveness found its home. He pressed his head against the stones and thought of her. For who knows where we go, he thought, although some might say the ultimate destiny of rich and poor, king and slave, was exactly the same. It was as if man's fate was to go into a corner where two stone walls met, whether slowly or quickly, and once he got to that corner, that was it. The end. And if by some special dispensation the crack opened and the walls parted, what was the destiny of the traveler when that happened, when the walls parted—what was there? An abyss. So there was no gain—either the end by the wall, or the abyss beyond the wall.

He heard Happy walking slowly up the steps—or was it finally, finally, finally, Zoe? He took Happy into his arms and kissed her. We have this place all to ourselves, he said. Look at the view! There's the Redentore Church all lit up. And to himself he thought: Who will I take up here twenty-five years from now? Slowly, he took off her clothes. She shivered.

"I'm cold," she said. "It's cold up here."

"Soon it won't be."

He made sure he faced the city and she faced the sea, just as he and Zoe had twenty-five years ago.

They walked down the tower steps together but did not say a word. He felt her distancing.

"What's the matter?" he said outside.

"You're not with me."

"That's exactly what I was thinking about you."

"You're not with me, Tommy. I can sense it. I got good antennas. You're with her, the other one, the one you were waiting for who didn't show up. A girl can tell these things."

"I'm with you. With you. With no one else."

"You're not. And that upsets me. And I don't believe you. And that upsets me even more."

"Then why did you screw me so beautifully upstairs?"

"What's one thing got to do with the other? That's one thing and this is another."

He felt he was losing her. He didn't want to lose her. There was a real love and a phantom love. There was a handful of wheat and a banquet in one's dream. There was Happy and there was Zoe.

"Come back to my room," he said. "I'm with you, Happy, and no one else. . . . I want you to be mine."

"I'll always be yours," she said. "No matter what."

He liked that.

"Like my gypsy mother used to say. Destiny plays itself out. Whatever is fated to be will surely be. No escaping what's in the crystal ball. But you're still in the doghouse with me."

"Why?"

"For barking up the wrong tree."

7. Running Until He Bumps Into Di Rossi

In his room he asked if she wanted to shower with him.

No, I'll wait here, she said.

When he came out, she was gone. Not a trace of her. She had taken the plastic bag she'd come in with earlier. The absence in the room was immediate. He knew she had walked out just a moment ago. He even sensed the draft of the closing door, a minus suck of wind. He dressed quickly. He jumped into his trousers and tugged, zipped, no need for socks, found his sneakers. A shirt would be enough, he figured, and buttoned it as he ran down the stairs. He could easily give chase under the Piazza arcades or around the tables. By now the night life would be winding down. Waiters were turning chairs on tables to scrub down their area of the square. Some waiters stood in the classic pose, crisp linen napkin on forearm, staring out at the thinning crowd, doing what they were best at—waiting.

Into the calles, whose silence always amazed him, as did the graphic darkness. An occasional naked bulb hanging from a wall gave out more gloom than light. He trotted, following what? Whom? But he knew she was near. He would catch her. She wouldn't disappear on him. He wouldn't let her go. He would be nice to her. He'd stop thinking of Zoe. He wouldn't give her cause to run away.

Now he moved even quicker. The cobblestones sped under his feet. The sound of his footfalls made him think of a B movie where a lone man, or woman, was being pursued, and hearts stop as the audience fears for the safety of the hunted man. In sympathy with the actor, his heart began to pound. But he wasn't hunted; he was hunting. Why couldn't he hear her? Why didn't she make a sound? She was floating, the wraith. There, there was the edge of her white skirt billowing across a little bridge, off to the right, faint must smell of water, gondoliers making their way home after a long day and night of celebration, the soft music of the oars lapping water to the rhythm of the opening bars of Vivaldi's "Winter". But when he crossed, he saw nothing. She must know the byways of Venice already. Him it had taken a long time to plumb the other Venice, off the Grand Canal, away from the Piazza San

Marco. The other Venice, Venetian Venice, the Venice of the mazes. Pasted in his mind was that map of the other Venice. But how did Happy know it? He went to the little pensione where she worked. The night clerk shrugged. She disappeared into thin air, he said. Not even a paper of hers left, he said. *Niente*, he said.

Rounding a corner, he saw a woman dressed in black, black blouse, long black skirt, black slouch hat, narrow black kerchief, leaning against the corner of a house. She neither moved nor said a word. But when approached, she made a couple of suggestive sounds to him. Maybe in Venetian dialect her "Tch, tch, tch" was the whore's cry for her wares. He passed her quickly, almost running, yes, running now but not moving aimlessly. Another little square opened up. In it stood a little fountain, water bubbling from the mouth of a cherubic boy. An old man sat on the ledge, looking like Rodin's thinker. The man greeted him, as if looking forward to a little relaxed conversation after the hectic night. What to do now? Tom imagined he was in a sentimental movie, and why not? All of Venice had that romantic, happy patina, except perhaps if you were in that obscure 19th century novella about the plague in Venice by Omasso Uomo that had recently achieved a cult following. But in that heart-warming, for-general-audiences family-oriented motion picture admired by all, when he came back home—surprise, surprise, come, zoom in camera, music up and over—she would be waiting for him, a clever little smile on her face, saying, See what I've done? Surprised you, right? I'll bet you never would have thought I'd do it, and he'd say, wisely, *Au contraire*, that's just the way I imagined it; in fact, I scripted this as I was walking back. You mean, she said, were she clever enough to think in convoluted layers, fusing a dream future with a questionable present, that my actions were predetermined, that I had no choice, that I was forced to come back, just because you formed the thought in your mind? No, not forced, he'd say. Destined. You did what you were destined to do. What your heart told you to do. You weren't following a script. You were following your heart.

And Happy falls into his arms with a little ecstatic cry. It was she, he decided. Masked, to fool me. He ran back to the corner where the woman in black had been, saw she was no longer there. Near the corner where she had stood, he asked some young men if they had seen or knew the woman of the night dressed in black. They didn't know. They hadn't seen her. There's no woman like that here, they said. We would know if there were. You can't hide something like that. There's never been women like that here. Their quarter didn't have women like that. The local priests were against it. The residents too. If there were women like that here, they'd be chased away. Like, like, the fellow looked for an apt image to make his point. Like, like a stranger, who doesn't belong here. And he gave out a laugh. But it was hard to tell if he was joking or being nasty.

Suddenly, while walking through a calle, he thought he saw salt or sugar crystals flying in the air. They landed on his head. Hail, he saw. Hailstones in summer! They bounded on the sidewalk, as if the sidewalk were the source of the hail, spitting them up from between the cobblestones. He crossed a little bridge, watching the hailstones land in the canal, bringing bits of light into the water. Then, as quickly as it had begun, by the time he went into another calle, the hail was done.

Now he was absolutely alone on the street. His trail of Happy lost. Maybe she was already on her way out of Venice. Picked up her suitcase and fled. On a train to God knows where. How come women were so disloyal and volatile, so fickle, so flighty and fleeting? He ran along a canal. At one point the water mirrored buildings and bridges with such photographic precision it was hard to tell which way was up, which down.

He began to sprint to the train station. Not many trains departed after midnight. She had planned this with malice aforethought. Not even a ponytail or shoe to trace her by. From the Accademia a vaporetto would get him to the station quickly, but he had dashed out without his wallet. Still, he could jump on a vaporetto. Chances were slim that the conductor would ask him for the fare; he'd assume he had a pass like most riders. But being caught without a ticket meant a ten-fold fine. At the train station, he'd run up and down all the platforms until he found her. It wouldn't be too difficult at this hour of the night. What a scene of reconciliation it would be, embracing on the platform, or he jumping up the step into the car, holding on to the railing just as the train was starting to chug-chug away and the mournful whistle of the locomotive was keening through the station, he sounding like an authentic Italian asking her, Why did you run away? Why? Why? Why? *Perché? Perché? Perché?*

I'm not running away, I just need a break, I have to think, you're older than me.

Not by much, was his response. You yourself said you could live with it.

Yes, but still it's a big gap. Give me time.

Okay, but not space. I want you near me. I don't want you to run away and me have to catch you at the last minute like I'm doing now, jumping aboard a moving train like they do in the movies.

But you see, she said proudly, you did find me, so I can't really get away from you after all.

Hey, wait a minute. Let's not forget it was *you* who ran off, remember? and I had to run practically naked all across the city to find you here. Do you have a ticket?

Yes.

In other words, you planned this escape a long time ago.

It's an open ticket, she said by way of excuse. I've had it a long time. She lowered her voice. Here comes the conductor, she warned him. Do *you* have a ticket?

Ticket? he said. I ran out so quickly I don't even have my wallet.

The calle were magically deserted as he trotted from one lane to another. But as he crossed one bridge a gray-bearded man wearing a black fedora and old-fashioned glasses that Spinoza might have ground stood at the bottom step as if waiting for him. As Tom walked around him, the man stuck out his foot and tripped him. Then he helped him up and brushed off his shirt.

"Thanks, but, um, it seems to me you tripped me."

"Who, me?" The man rubbed his short, clipped beard. "Oh, no. Not me."

"You didn't purposely stick your foot out?"

"No."

"But I saw your foot out."

"Then why did you trip? If you saw my foot that was allegedly out?"

"I saw it on my way down."

"Impossible! I did not trip you. No and no again."

"Come on! I don't believe it. You don't look like a nasty man. Why did you trip me? What for?"

"I did not trip . . . well . . . on second thought . . . okay, yes, I did."

"But why?"

"For your own good. To save you time. You were too much in a hurry."

"Is that a reason to trip someone? I'm in a rush. I have to meet a girl who disappeared on me."

"Forget her. If she disappears, she disappears. Vanished is vanished. Gone, gone. That's what I'm trying to tell you. Like the prayer book says: Run to do good deeds, not to pursue women."

"It's not women. It's just one woman. Mine."

The man looked at him patiently, innocently. Tom didn't move.

"Wait a minute, signore," Tom said. "You look familiar."

"Could be. I've been around Venice a long long time." He put out his hand. "Let me introduce myself. I'm Azariah di Rossi, the Chief Rabbi of Venice. Maybe you've seen me during my evening strolls. At night I like to get out of the ghetto and walk around the city."

"How long have you been rabbi here?"

"Three hundred thirty three years."

"Three hundred thirty three years! That's a long time to keep one job."

"Yes. Another thirteen and I'll have tenure. But this is my second position. I was even longer in my first one. I was rabbi in Rome for, oh, God knows, hundreds and hundreds of years." Now he whispered. "I even got to know Julie."

"Andrews?"

"No. Caesar. . . . And once, for a fundraiser, I even did a routine with Caesar."

"Julie?"

"No. Sid."

The rabbi adjusted the glasses on is nose. "You like them? Interesting, no? Baruch Spinoza made them for me. . . . Here, look, I want to show you something." He pulled out of his pocket a little oil painting rolled into a scroll. "See? A portrait of me by Canaletto. I'm sitting on my gondola, on my way to officiate at

Sabbath services at the Scuola Tedesca. . . . I know what you're going to say. But in those days it was the only way to get to the synagogue on Sabbath, so riding on a gondola on Sabbath was permitted to get to services."

"Excuse me," Tom said. "It's been very nice meeting you and I'm impressed by the Canaletto but I have to get moving. I'll be late. She'll be gone."

"Hold it! That's why I tripped you. Sometimes if you're late you're just on time. And, anyway, trust me, she's no good for you."

"But you don't even know her."

"I don't have to know her. Did you know her three weeks ago?"

"No."

"Neither did I. So we're even."

"I really have to go now." Tom tried moving forward but felt a barrier of wind blocking his way.

"Did you read 'The Aleph' by Italo Calvodka?" the rabbi asked.

"I'm not familiar with Calvodka."

"But you speak Italian so fluently."

Tom shrugged. He didn't want to correct the all-knowing rabbi that 'The Aleph' wasn't written by Calvodka.

"Calvodka shows us there that the world is full of inexplicable mysteries. That's what I want to show you."

"Thanks a lot. Now I've lost two women."

"What do you mean two? First it's one, now it's two? Maybe I should trip you again and you'll lose your harem."

"It's too complicated. One woman from long ago was supposed to show up. We made an appointment and she didn't come. Now this one has vanished and you made me lose her. So I got to go before it's too late. Why am I standing here talking to you?"

"Maybe it will help you find her. Read 'The Aleph'. Sometimes you find things you never lost. And vice versa. But if you do find her, you'll lose her. It's only if you don't find her that she'll be yours."

"I want to find her. I don't go for fairy-tale mysticism."

"Your choice."

"Can you tell me where I'll find her and when?"

"Don't worry. It will take as long as it takes and not one second more. You'll be just in time. I stopped the clock."

"Everyone here seems to be stopping the clock tonight."

"You mean my friends Tall Maria and Jack the Gondolier?"

"You know them too?"

"You live in a city for three hundred thirty-three years and you get to know almost everyone."

"So you have a stop watch too."

"Like in your football—you're American, yes? I can tell by your accent . . . on women—I stopped the clock. Time isn't moving now. So if she's going to catch a train, it won't leave. You heard of Joshua in the Bible?"

"Yes."

"Well, he stopped the sun. Stopped time."

"You can do that?"

"That's child play. Anyone who's been a rabbi more than thirty-nine years can do that."

"Show me."

"If I'm not mistaken, your name isn't Gideon, right?"

"I don't understand."

"You know Joshua but you don't know Gideon?"

"I didn't get up to the G's. Introduce me."

"When God spoke to Gideon about leading the fight against the Midianites, he demanded proof. Are you Gideon?"

"No."

"And you're not Moses either, if I'm not mistaken."

"He also demanded proof?"

"Yes. From God when he told him to tell Pharaoh, Let my people go."

"Are you God?"

"God forbid!. . . . But I do my best. . . . Okay, now that you have stopped, now that you're not in such a hurry, go, and you'll find her. But it still won't do you any good."

Tom thought of walking around the rabbi seven times for good luck but decided against it. Everyone is such a pessimist around here, it might do more harm than good.

"So long," he said and trod off.

But he didn't get too far. Azariah di Rossi tripped him again.

"Why'd you do that?" he asked the rabbi, who was helping him up again.

"Three reasons. One for good luck. Two, this time it was my left foot—we love to balance things out in Venice—and three, I wanted you to have a good trip."

Tom stood. The rabbi brushed him off once more, an act whose play on words was not lost on Tom.

"Is the clock still stopped?"

"Stopped. Dead in its tracks. In case you're off to the train."

Tom had told neither man nor man of God what he had done years back. But since this was a stranger, a chance encounter in the night, he now confessed what he had done to Zoe.

Azariah di Rossi said nothing, neither reprimand or consolation.

"Is that why you were waiting for me? Because you knew?"

The rabbi did not reply.

"Is that why you tripped me?"

The Chief Rabbi of Venice looked at him as if he were speaking a foreign tongue.

"And I never asked if the child was a boy or a girl. What do you think?"

"In my hundreds of years, I found that the chances are about fifty-fifty. Maybe fifty-two, forty-eight, if the weather is good."

"Which way?"

"Both. But you look like a vigorous man."

"Man forms part of my name—Manning."

"See? A person like you would father male children."

"So it's a boy, you think."

"Very likely," the rabbi said. "Most probably a boy."

"I think so too," said Tom.

"But on the other hand, it could also most probably be a girl—and maybe even—"

"Maybe even what? Is there a third choice?"

"Three, four? Who knows? We got a bargain basement of choices out there now. We live in a modern world, like my optician Baruch Spinoza used to say . . . . You're not Jewish, right?

"You're right on that one, rabbi. But I have—had—some religious affiliation. My parents are Friends."

"That's nice. I admire that. They should be. Married couples should be friends. It makes for happy marriages. I've been married now, let's see, we celebrated our six-hundred eighty ninth wedding anniversary a few years ago."

"The Friends are a religious designation in America. They're Quakers. You heard of that?"

Azariah di Rossi rolled the sound in his mouth soundlessly.

"Quaker?" the rabbi pronounced it in the European way, Kvaaaacker, like a duck quacking. Then added:

"Your parents worship oats?"

Now he slowed down. With time stopped, what's the use of running? He walked the dark calles and across the bridges with their murky light. He walked in the dark, embracing the silence of the lanes. The only sounds he heard were his own footfalls on the cobblestones.

By the right column of steps at the railroad station, where, had he been in front of the New York Public Library, the lion would have been, he saw a bundle of black clothing. Black skirt, black blouse, black floppy hat.

It must be the streetwalker's clothes. But how could that be? He had seen her at the corner in an inner courtyard and then dashed over bridges to the station. She couldn't have possibly outrun him.

On the broad steps of the train station young people, students, fake students, travelers, pseudo-artistes, slick beggars and bums were sprawled out on this warm heart of the night to save a night's lodging. He had to make his way around them like an obstacle course. He asked a group of youngsters, Have you seen a pair of red shoes and a green sweater floating by? They missed the last two words and told him they'd found nothing that was lost.

He came into the terminal blinking at the lights. The platforms were deserted. Happy was not there. He went back out. He felt that an entire crowd of youngsters was staring at this distraught man walking the steps like some kind of automaton, as if performing for them on the great stage of Venice. But he didn't care. If you had what I had, folks, and then lost it, you'd be tearing up and down the tracks too.

Well, pop, did you find your red shoes? said a young red-bearded chap lying on the bottom step. An ironic glimmer accompanied the question, as if he were mocking Tom and his outré red shoes which no civilized man ever wore in Venice, except maybe during Carnivale. Tom did not reply. With Happy gone, Venice lost its luster, for Venice had a feel to it, unique to each person. Something like the waves of love you give to someone and she sends them back to you. But with Happy gone, Venice became a different place; an ether of gloom seeped into every crevice of the city. He went straight home. The door to his room was still open. She wasn't there. The smile he imagined, See? surprised you, right? wasn't there.

He lay down to rest but fell asleep, dreamt of train stations and endless train rides in endless tunnels. He slept fitfully. But woke completely refreshed.

He had slept only seven minutes.

8. Where'd You Disappear To?

Happy had forgotten her red shoes under his bed, he saw. But how could she have gone out without her shoes? Maybe she had another pair of walking shoes in her bag and had worn those and forgotten these. He placed them next to the door. If Happy didn't return tomorrow he'd bring the shoes to her pensione. Perhaps she'd write and ask her boss to mail them to her. My God, he thought, she never even asked my address. I'll leave the pensione my address too when I return the shoes. I'll give the clerk a tip and ask him to include my note when he mails the shoes back.

As he straightened up he felt a sensation he had never had before, a strange pressure on his bladder, as if hands were pressing his lower abdomen. He went to the bathroom. When he came out, her red shoes were on the bed, pointing up, standing against the iron bars of the bed frame. What was going on here? Was it his eyes or was his memory going? It was late. Too late. Time had been suspended and, compressed in a mass, it lay heavily on him. Now he understood the expression about the heaviness of time. Only when it flowed unimpeded was it thin as air, light as snow. When it stopped, it turned to ice, to stone; it placed him halfway between today and tomorrow, in a region not night, not dawn. And then there was this urge to pee again. Who pulled the plug to his pecker? As he flushed he heard a stirring in his room. When he opened the door, he saw a strange sight, or at least he thought he saw a strange sight, for in retrospect he couldn't tell if he really saw what he saw or if he had had a waking dream.

In the mist of his imagination he remembered seeing one red shoe running around the room and then what appeared to be a wig, a head of hair. And then the apparition stood still.

Oh, my God, he thought. It's Happy. She's forgotten the last word.

Kinnercadoo, he shouts at her.

And then remembered that she can't hear him anyway. The hair moved back and forth as if she were saying, No. Was it no to his kinnercadoo, or was she shaking her head because she couldn't remember the fourth word of the formula.

Next thing he remembered was the sound of his bathroom

door shutting and Happy on his bed. The shoes in that same position, upended against the iron bars of the bed frame, as if she had just slipped into them. She was wearing what she had worn before, but there was a narrow black silk kerchief around her neck.

"Where did you disappear to?"

"With disappearing," she said calmly, "there's no where. There's just why, maybe how."

"Okay. Why?"

"I was mad at you. I told you before. I didn't like it that you didn't want to take me to the fountain to meet your girl friend."

He banged his fists on the mattress — less painful than smashing the wall. "Dammit! I told you I don't have a girl friend. Why don't you let me explain? Why do you make assumptions on your own and then act on them as if they were absolute facts?"

"I don't make assumptions. Up in the tower you weren't with me. I told you that. When me and you are together I want all of you, not half of you. I don't want you thinking of someone else when you're with me. Every time you think of someone else I'll disappear."

He tried to make light of it. "Hmm, that gives me lots of power over you, doesn't it?"

She didn't say.

"You still angry?"

"I'm here, aren't I?"

He didn't bother correcting her dumb south Albany English. "Meaning what?"

"Meaning I forgive you."

Who was she to forgive him? he thought. Wasn't forgiveness a two-way street? He still had to forgive her for running away from him and causing him anguish, making him run around Venice half the night. This nasty side of her showed him that perhaps it wasn't Zoe who had arranged that assault. In fact, maybe it was Happy. But then, why did she save him? Why? Because it was all part of the plan—punishment and salvation.

"So it was you who arranged that kidnapping?"

"Maybe."

Who are you to shape my life? he was about to say. He looked at her. There was anger in her eyes but charm as well. How could you dislike a delectable face like hers? He loved her now frizzy blonde hair which she had done a week ago. Trouble was that Happy was right. But of course he wouldn't admit it to her. She had sensed it with that sixth or seventh sense that women have, that eighth or ninth sense that witches have, that in the tower he was thinking about Zoe, and she complained. Would he like it if she were thinking about another guy while he was screwing her?

"And maybe not."

He shook his head. "You're a mystery. How did you disappear so quickly? One moment you're here, the next you're not."

"Exactly. That's how the magic books define invisibility. I made myself invisible again."

"How?"

"First, I disguised myself, then I vanished into thin air. . . . Why is your mouth open like that? You don't believe me?"

"I thought you only become invisible for an emergency."

"This was an emergency.... Still don't believe me?"

"After what I've seen today, I'm ready to believe anything." He paused a while, considering what he said. Sometimes words take shape and fly before the will has censored them. "Where'd you learn the trick? I'll bet in some exotic place like Nepal."

"Try Albany. My gypsy grandmother taught my mother and she taught me."

"What did your grandmother use it for?"

"Same thing I used it for it just now. To get away from my grandfather. And then, when I was old enough, my mom taught me. And to me only."

"And not to your brother?"

"I don't have a brother."

"And if you had one?"

"She wouldn't of taught him."

"Why?"

"Because this is passed down from mother to daughter. And, anyway, man's ectoplasm is too heavy. Only women can disappear."

"Plenty of husbands disappear."

Happy laughed. "But not with the help of magic."

"I'd like to know the formula."

"So you can disappear on me?"

"No. That I can do without magic. But I'd like to know the

formula. Can you tell me the formula for becoming invisible?"

She said no. But she didn't look sorry, apologetic or contrite. She didn't look down as she said it. Didn't even pretend to be sorry with a false sad smile. She looked him straight in the eye with that no. "If I tell it, I lose it. But I can tell you it's three special words."

"And those same three words make you visible again?"

She shook her head, rolled her eyes, as if complaining against some unseen authority. "That's the problem. *That* formula, I told you once, is four words and I keep forgetting the last word and that's dangerous. That's why I don't make myself invisible."

"But you just said you did."

"I was quoted out of context. What I meant was, as often as I'd like to."

"Explain, please. You're telling everything in half words."

"No one can help me when I'm invisible. The answer has to come from within me. That's the way magic works. It has its own rules, its own logic, and it's not simple. People think that magic is simple, hocus pocus abracadabra and all that. It's not. It's complex and full of hard work. Physical and spiritual preparation. So before I make myself invisible I have to be absolutely sure I know all four return words—otherwise, if I forget one of them, I'm finished. Invisible forever."

He said what he had said about believing anything she said, but upon reflection concluded that he really didn't believe his words and believed hers even less. He was teasing with his questions, at least he hoped he was, being ironic, like the fellow at the railway station who asked him if he had found his lost red shoes. But Tom's voice didn't give him away. Why was he hesitating, wasting time? There were more adventures destined for this long and timeless day, a day that was nearly over and had hardly begun. What kind of nonsensical conversation was he being drawn into anyway, invisibility!?

"And why did you move out so quickly from your hotel?"

"Who says I moved out of my hotel?"

"I asked the clerk there and that's what he said. He said you were gone."

"Did you ever hear of the Tell-him-I'm-not-home message? They just told you what I told them to tell you."

"What a bitch!" he exploded.

"A hurt bitch. You don't seem to understand that. When I'm not hurt I'm not a bitch."

"We're fighting again. And we shouldn't be." He dropped his voice, sculpted a sweet, moderate, almost whispery tone that would show his sincerity. "I have no girl friend. This was a meeting with a friend of mine from back home that I arranged a long time ago. Didn't you hear what I told Jack Benny?"

"So how come you were thinking of her while you were screwing me in the Tower?"

"Stop it!"

"And why didn't you want me along? You're ashamed of me."

"On the contrary. At the concert I was looking around, proud of how other men were admiring your beauty."

"Really?"

"Honest and truly. Didn't you see me looking around?"

"Yes. But I thought you were looking for her."

"Again that mythical 'her'! Come off it! I told you. Only you. I have eyes only for you. Come here." He spread his arms.

She fell into them. He clasped her, held her tight. He put his lips to hers. The reunion brought no music in the background but it was sweet nevertheless. He felt her pressing up to him with a warmth she had lacked in the Bell Tower.

He thought of that lovemaking again. It puzzled him, it annoyed him, that she could make love so coolly, without emotion, so dis-attached. But now she held his face, ran her fingers from his neck to his arms and kissed him. Her eyes were closed. Warmth and love flowed from her to him.

"Come," he said. "I have a surprise for you. We're going to conclude this Festa night the way Venetians have done for centuries."

It was too late for the Danieli, he thought. Soon it will be dawn. The Danieli caper would have to wait for some other time.

Happy took off her black neckerchief and put it in her bag.

9. About Face

"What's the surprise?" she said.

"If I tell you, it won't be a surprise."

"But if you tell me, I'll be surprised. Come on, tell me. I'll enjoy the surprise even more if I know it in advance."

Imitating a vamp, she drew close and raised one shoulder provocatively. She brushed her index finger lightly over his cheek, down to his neck and chest. She ran her tongue slowly over her upper lip and, fixing her eyes on his, smiled as if mocking her own teasing.

"All right." He sighed. "We're going to see the sunrise on the Lido. It's a tradition here on Festa night." One he hadn't observed with Zoe, he remembered. Because he didn't know about it then. One can't know everything. If I'd known about it, Zoe, I would have taken you to the Lido instead of going to sleep.

She was about to ask a question but he answered it before she spoke.

"Don't worry. We won't have to walk on water. . . . Tonight is the only night of the year the vaporettos run all night long."

He packed a blanket into a duffel bag; she took her pocketbook. They entered the packed vaporetto. Tom stared down into the lagoon. In the gray water made slate by the dark and by the dull light of thick, white-edged clouds, little amoeba-shaped rounds of water darted like nervous insects, interlocking, shining, pulsating with even greater nervousness as they neared the ferry. He kept staring at the movement of the water, which took the predawn light of the sky and broke it into thousands of little vibrating components. To him they looked like creatures that seemed to be alive. But was he alive? he asked the water. Why didn't you come, Zoe, and give me life?

But then remembered that that was then and now it's now. Remember what your father said about wheat in hand and phantom banquets? He had a life to live today. Yesterday—kiss it goodbye. Maybe it's better she didn't come. Now he could focus on what he had and not what he didn't have or could have had. He looked at Happy walking beside him and felt better.

From the vaporetto station they walked to the beach. It was

early dawn. In front of the Hotel Excelsior they saw an endless line of chairs and cabanas. Tom slowed down, inspected the chairs.

"That's the one," he said and bowed. "I think."

"What are you doing?" Happy asked. "I thought you wanted to take a long walk on the beach."

"I did. I do. But now I'm paying homage."

"To a chair?" Her voice rose.

"Not really to a chair, but to the person who once used it. Call it a kind of literary pilgrimage. . . . Did you ever hear of Aschenbach?"

"No. I heard of Johann Bach."

Thanks to me, he thought. "This one is a writer." Tom paused, closed his eyes for a moment. "I *think* it's Aschenbach. Maybe Eschenbach. . . . My God, I'm blanking out. Let's see, Gustav Eschenbach . . . or is it Wolfram Aschenbach, his son by a different father?"

"Don't ask me," Happy said. "When is the sun gonna rise? I'm tired. . . . And anyway, what's it got to do with this chair?"

"This is where he died . . . . Let's see, maybe there's a plaque on one of these chairs. He had just finished his famous book, *Parting in Venice*, or is it *Partying in Venice*?" Tom stopped, glared at Happy. "What's the matter with you? Why can't you remember a thing?"

"He must have made a great impression on you," Happy said carefully. Her eyes smiled but not her lips.

"It's not so much his book or even the man himself . . . but the fact that he died writing, pen in hand, *that's* what impressed me. . . . What a way for a writer to go! It's like a sailor going down with his ship. Or a bus driver dying at the wheel as he slowly goes over a cliff. Or a painter at the easel. A lawyer, or a poet, at the bar. It's so fitting. Dying while you're doing what you're supposed to do."

The morning was already warm. A moist, salty breeze from the sea. Fingers of pink spread in the sky. Soon the sun would rise. Only he and Happy walked along the beach, hand in hand, seigneurs of their little desert island, until they found a quiet place, away from view of the large hotels.

Tom spread the blanket and wrapped it around himself with Happy. She reached for her bag and pulled out a tissue. You cold?

he asked her. Not with you, she said. He put his arms around her; she pressed up against him. At once she began to kiss him. Her body radiated heat, in tune with him. It began with parted lips and puffs of quickened breath. He found her breasts and kissed them. The sand molded itself to their bodies. Through a veil, he saw the horizon moving up and down, up and down, as if he were a ship at sea, until it rested, removed from the sunrise.

I'm happy, he thought, the word like a sunrise in his mind. When had he last been happy? He could not say. The feeling was a warm, child-like bliss. He no longer missed Zoe. Zoe was far away. Now he had Happy. Now, he thought, the time had come. Now he could begin a normal life.

"I missed you. When you ran away, I was frantic that I'd lost you. I didn't think I could, I didn't think I would, but I've fallen in love."

"Really?" she said. "With whom?"

Let her have her little joke, he thought.

"A girl I know."

"The one you waited for and didn't show?" And she gave that tongue in cheek little smile that said: I'm joking—but I still know a thing or two.

Little witch, he thought. But you're adorable.

"The girl I waited for did show up. That's the one I love."

He gazed at her, waited. The sea did not move. Waves stood still in mid-break, like in a picture. Faint tints of the coming sunrise skimmed the surface, a muted rainbow. But still the sea was green and dark, unbroken by skiff or gull.

The pause before she spoke hurt him. But when she said what she said next, the quick hurt went quickly away.

"I love you too," she said. "But you know that."

"That's just what an agamous man like me wanted to hear."

He pulled a ring out of his pocket, a cheap little ring, an unpretentious little thing, a little ding-a-ling of a little ring, more a symbol than a ring, and slowly put it on her finger.

"I never thought it would happen to me. Wanting a girl to be with the rest of my life."

"Are you marrying me?"

"In a way." Then he amended to it: "This instant. Now. At once. *Immediamente*."

"The formalities can wait, she says," Happy said brightly.

"I'm so happy with you, I can't believe it."

"I'm Happy without you," she countered.

"Back to the Shakespearean puns of our first meeting. . . . No. Really. But I have such strange feelings sometimes. Maybe I'm not even me! Isn't it possible that I'm not me? That I'm only a puppet put here by someone else's thoughts?"

"Yes," Happy said. "Mine!"

"That everyone," he continued, paying no attention to her remark, "that everyone is real around me except me."

"If I wish it."

"That what happened to me," he said hopefully, "didn't happen to me. That what I did to others that may have hurt them wasn't really done because it was all a dream."

"Fat chance," she said flatly, with not one ounce of humor or compassion in her voice.

Her next remarks surprised him, for he'd never thought she would express herself in such an imaginative way. It was as though someone else were speaking, not she.

She said, "It's possible that on the Piazza, among the hundreds of people you pass today, you will meet someone who isn't real, but a figment of someone's imagination, a work of fiction. He will look real, not stiff as a mask or dumb as a manikin. But if you speak to him, he won't be able to answer. But it's not you. No, it won't be you. You're real and whatever you are and have done is real." She yawned. "Why are we talking so much? I'm sleepy."

"Sleep, darling. Close your eyes. I'll wake you up at sunrise."

"What's 'agamous'?" she muttered before she fell asleep.

He stroked her hair, her cheeks, her arms and breasts. She fell asleep in his arms. He looked at her. She looked like a baby in that child-like, blissful sleep, her soft, smooth skin like an infant's. He felt so good he could have embraced all of Venice with one hug. How lucky I am, he thought, to be so happy. Happy stirred, gave a little moan. Shh, he said. Bad dreams go away. Away go bad dreams. Dreams away bad go, the thrice-said charm, just like his Scottish grandma had taught him during childhood when he would awake from a nightmare. He thought Happy would wake but she curled even closer into herself like a baby. Then she turned and lay on her back, arms in the surrender position. Like in a medieval painting, where a pointing finger draws your eye elsewhere on the canvas, Happy's finger pointed to her pocketbook. The bag was still open. He wanted to close it, touch it, put it away, do something with it. Just then he felt a wave-like force invading him, not unlike the wave that separated them last night, or the wave of good health that came over him when tall Maria cured him, a sudden wave of invisible light that was not light but more the darkness in the sea sweeping over him like a transparent shadow, and a sense of gloom, blue black in hue and spreading like fine sand in his veins.

He looked at Happy's face. Saw his face in hers, her face in his. It was one. They are one. They will be one. Then little lines of force, as if from a magnet, a message he could not resist, sent his hand to her bag. He didn't know what made him do it, but the force of that suction he could not withstand.

The mirror, the magic mirror, or perhaps something else beckoned him. More than beckoned. Pointed the way. Her finger the guide. He went into her pocketbook. There was her black silk kerchief and the little black velvet bag with the magic mirror. He took it out and looked into it. Saw his face. A face not masked and not unmasked. Then turned the looking-glass upside down. And as if he were in a Chagall painting, there he was, upside down, his chin at the top of the reflection, his hair at the bottom. He didn't dare turn the glass again. But he did look away toward the horizon, searching for the coming sun, wondering if the reverse image would still be there. He remembered Happy saying that in the mirror one could only see one's image upside down once, not twice. He decided not to test it. For what if there would be no image there at all? That would mean, as folktales have it, that he would die. And even if it weren't so, and there would be no no-image in the glass, he didn't want to spoil that special moment he had just witnessed, for how many unique moments are there in one's lifetime? Without looking again, he slipped the little mirror back into the black velvet bag. It was then—it must have fallen there when he pulled out the mirror—that he saw her driver's license on the sand.

He held her license, saw her name, her age.

A buzz of chills started down his face, then spread like little dots to every inch of his scalp. Now he didn't know if he was rightside up or upside down.

He woke her with an urgency, an inevitability like sunrise.

She blinked, was suddenly awake.

"What's the matter?"

"What's that little black kerchief sticking out of your bag?" he asked her—but that wasn't the question he wanted to ask.

"You saw me wearing it before. It's a good luck charm from my gypsy grandmother. If I carry it with me no harm can happen to me."

"And whoever is with you?"

"I hope, but I don't know. It seemed to help you too."

The vector in his heart was driving one way; his will another.

He approached carefully. This is what he wanted to ask:

"I just discovered something disturbing. . . . You told me you were thirty."

"Almost. In another month."

"That's not what your driver's license says. It says you're twenty-four. Why did you lie to me? I can't stand girls who lie about their age. Why'd you lie? Why? Why? Why?" he pleaded.

"Women lie about their age. You know that. My mother always told me to tell the truth and lie about my age. . . . Even Jack Benny lied about his age and everyone knew it. How come that doesn't bother you? Why did you look into my pocketbook? Why? Why? Why?"

"Your finger pointed to it. It said: Look in there. Seek and ye shall find the truth. It was you who led me to it."

"It isn't right, it isn't nice, it isn't moral and ethical to go into someone else's pockets. It's like being a pickpocket and I can't stand pickpockets."

"I'm not a pickpocket. You yourself told me anytime you want to look, it's yours."

"But only for the mirror. Not for anything else."

"Why didn't you tell me how old you really were?"

"Because I liked you, you dope. When you said you were thirty-nine, I said thirty because that put me in the same decade as you, so it was all right. Because if I'd said twenty-four you'd think I was a baby and leave me. . . . Remember the first or second time we walked up to the Rialto Bridge you stopped to catch your breath? It made me think that there were many years between us."

He hadn't stopped to catch his breath, he recalled. Where did she dig that up from? It was just a ploy. Suddenly, here, on the sand, at the cusp of sunrise, on the morning after he should have met Zoe, should have, because the conjunction of so many good things and great memories had taken place if not for something that had gone wrong; he couldn't imagine why she hadn't come, he suddenly thought of her again, whom he had banished from his mind. And now he wanted to be at the American Express office in Venice again. Perhaps she would emerge, as if she'd just gone in a moment ago with her army green knapsack, a poor-looking thing, pathetic even, compared to the satiny lightweight knapsacks that everyone carried. And now, twenty-five years later, he felt embarrassed for her, not only for the spilling of dozens of sundries that attracted everyone's attention and broke the mood in the room, but for the outré, out of fashion, army surplus knapsack probably from World War Two, from her daddy's time, that she carried with her on her shoestring hungry tour of Europe. It was Zoe he thought of now, not Happy, the Happy who flooded his mind, enveloping it, crushing it.

"I remember your father was an older man," he told her. "I get the feeling that your mother was too? Does she lie about her age?"

"Of course."

"And do you when asked how old she is?"

"No. She's sixty-two."

The relief that came over him was palpable. "That's good," he said. "That's very good. That's wonderful." A beneficent angel, that sixty-two-year-old mother. He felt the angel's wings stroking him, blessing him. He looked at Happy. She was right for him. He couldn't live without her. Look how often they separated but clicked back together again like magnets.

"By the way, what's her name?"

"Who?"

"Your mom."

"What difference does it make?"

"Why the reticence? Just tell me. You never told me her name."

"Did you tell me your mother's name? I'm just realizing it, I don't know anything about you. Not even your shoe size."

"Do you want to know?"

"Yes, of course."

"Size ten. With some brands nine-and-a-half."

"Not that, you dope, your mother's name."

"It's Mary Jane."

"And my mother's is Maria."

"Sounds familiar. Which Maria?"

"You know."

"I don't believe it! The tall one, here, in Venice, who cured me?"

"Uh-huh."

"She's your mother? You never told me you had a mother in Venice."

"Why do you think I'm spending so much time here? And who else would take you up to her home?"

"Then why didn't they give you a big hello, or you them?"

"Gypsies are not demonstrative in public. But she did say, 'Nice to see you,' remember?"

"So how come you didn't recognize the dog?"

"It was a new dog."

"And the triplets were new too, I suppose."

She didn't comment on that.

"Any other questions?"

"Plenty. How come Aunt Maria is so tall?"

"It's kilts."

"Kilts? Kilts don't make people tall."

"I said stilts. Don't you hear well?"

"It must be a bad connection. So it's stilts."

"Yes. Stilts. She used to be a crown."

"What's that got to do with it?"

"What's what got to do with it?"

"Crown. Crown and stilts."

"I didn't say crown. You must be going deaf. I said clown. She used to be a crown. That's why she wears kilts. . . ." Then a moment later she added, "I see you're still confused about my family.

Remember when I, like, asked a certain question, Maria lost her temper and snapped, 'Shall I ask you the secret of how you' —She almost let it slip but then caught herself in time."

"So if you knew them, how come you asked so many questions?"

"No more than you're asking now. And you know me too. You don't ask you don't learn."

"Then how come she got so sore when you asked so many questions?"

"For the same reason I'm getting sore with yours. Gypsy magicians are that way. They don't hold back. They always tell the truth."

"But about your staying in Venice. When we first met you told me a different story."

"Never believe a gypsy."

And she fell asleep again. Fast asleep, as though she'd never been woken up.

The violet sun tipped in the horizon.

11. Sunrise

"Wendy, get up! Wake up, Wendy!" She opened her eyes.

"So it is Wendy. First day we met you said you'd be bored to death with a name like that."

"I didn't lie. That's why I don't use it. How'd you know my name is Wendy?"

"I'm part gypsy too. How come you're named Wendy if you're called Happy?"

"Happy is the name I've gone by since I was a baby. Only my official papers have Wendy."

"Then why are you called Happy?"

"Because my mom was so glad to have me she called me Happy. . . . Why so glum? You'd rather I was called Dopey?"

"No, that's what I should be called."

"No, you should be called Grumpy."

"Then why were you named Wendy?"

"That's a long story. I have two mothers, my real one, who gave me the name Happy, and my biological mother. . . ."

"Oh, I see. A surrogate mother."

"No, I was adopted."

"You was what?"

"Adopted. Stop shouting!"

From somewhere far away, in a land where invisibility no longer matters, he asked her: "Do you know your real mother?"

"Yes. . . . No."

"What is that supposed to mean?"

"Depends on what you mean by knowing."

"But do you know who she is? Somebody from Albany, right?"

"No, but I know who she is."

"Do you remember her name?"

"Of course."

"What is it?"

"What difference does it make?"

Again that ridiculous question. "If it makes no difference, then tell me. What difference does it make?" he repeated and gave out a sarcastic laugh. "What difference? Plenty of difference. Tell me."

The word bubbled out of her mouth. He saw the sphere of the first letter breaking like a soap bubble, the speck of light falling, no, not falling, plummeting like a shattered star. Oh, for a pigeon to pluck the name from the mouth and with a flap of beating wings abscond. The missing fountain, away it went. The Bell Tower bent. Flood waters came and inundated the Piazza.

"Mary Jane," she said. "I told you we look alike, me and you. I told you you were my brother, remember?"

"Your words are like a prism," he told her. "One turn and I see a rainbow. Another—and I see plain glass."

"Gypsies talk like that. With transparent words. You provide the colors."

The sun, gauzed in crimson, topped over the horizon with an ambiguous glow.

He shook her awake.

Irritation cleared her mind quicker than espresso.

"Sunrise already? How many more times you gonna wake me? This is the fifth time already."

"Second."

"Let me sleep. Let me dream."

"I'm depressed. Agitated. Upset. And you want to dream. I want to live and you want to sleep. Help me. Help me overcome it. Only you can help me now. If you don't help me now I die."

"What's the matter?"

He figured he would start on a positive note. That's what his father had taught him. You start positive, you end positive. "I noticed you weren't born in March."

"Is that what's troubling you? There's lots of months I wasn't born in. Why the sigh of relief?"

"Because I don't like March. It's a fickle month."

"Yeah, I was born in February. . . ."

"A good month. One of the best."

". . . a bit premature."

From a sitting position he sank back to the sand. He still hadn't digested the mystery of her name. Her name, he sensed in his gut which did his thinking now, would explain everything.

"Can you clear up for me why you were named Wendy and who named you?"

"Wendy is the name my real mother gave me and. . . ."

"I thought your real mother gave you the name Happy."

"She did, but my real real mother named me Wendy."

"Wait a minute! I'm more confused than ever. You said Mary

Jane was your mother."

"That was just a joke."

"Then you said Maria was your mother and she didn't even seem to know you."

"Maria is just one of my godmothers."

She's lying through her teeth, he thought. Gypsies, she said—telling the truth just only once—always lie.

"God Almighty! How many do you have?"

"A few. Mothers, that is. All gypsy children have at least two. One who gave them birth, the other who raised them, a third, a favorite godmother. . . ."

Oh God, there came those chills again, pinpricks like a machine all over his body. Now he knew what the prisoner felt in the puncturing machine in Kafka's "The Penal Colony."

"So who is your real real mother?"

"The one who gave birth to me before she put me up for adoption. . . . Any other questions?"

"Do you know your real real mother?"

"Not really. Why you asking me all this?"

"Adopted kids rarely know their real mothers."

"Not nowadays."

"So you do know her. Have you met her?"

"No. I could have but I chickened out. I didn't want to be split in half. So I spoke to her. Once. On the phone. And that was it."

"What's her real name?"

He waited for the *What's the difference?* but it didn't come.

"Mrs. Greyson."

He barely uttered the words, "I mean her first name," as if chunks of dough were in back of his throat, blocking the sounds.

"What difference does it make?"

Should he explain to her the difference? Were there words enough in the English language, in the entire *Unabridged* that would suffice to explain what difference it would make?

She began to speak.

The fountain moved. It came and went. Around and around he spun around it, seven times.

The wine red sun now thralled over the horizon. Happy's face was reflected in the umber light. Now, finally, the awaited sunrise suffused sky and sea, surf and sand, with blood orange light.

She said:

"Zoe."